PRAISE FOR *A GUEST IN THE JUNGLE*

"A *Romancing the Stone* in print."

—*Pittsburgh Post*

"With this novel, James Polster moves to the cutting edge of a new crop of talented West Coast writers."

—*San Francisco Review of Books*

"Hilarious and unpredictable...best of all, a clear message about the evils of tropical rainforest destruction—a wonderful book and highly recommended."

—*World Rainforest Report*

"Polster's book is so engrossing, unpretentious, and uproariously funny that the reader may not recognize at first how poetically written and beautifully crafted it is...You can't put this book down. If you try, it will follow you through every room in the house."

—*Bob Scher, The South American Explorer*

"An action-packed comedy with blazing insights into life strewn along the trail."

—*Cleveland Plain Dealer*

"A thriller that is both frightening and funny, Polster's impressive ability to evoke the jungle in all its perilous beauty gives the reader a real sense of being there."

—*Los Angeles Daily News*

"The diversity of life, both wild and human, is incredible, but a very hard reality comes through—the big reality, the big question."

"Polster's deadpan wit makes the twists and turns of his clever books a joy to read."

"Polster practices the humorist's craft with a bold, sure hand that recalls Mark Twain."

A Guest in the Jungle

A Guest in the Jungle

A NOVEL BY JAMES POLSTER

PUBLISHED BY

amazon encore

Published by AmazonEncore
P.O. Box 400818
Las Vegas, NV 89140

ISBN-13: 9781935597513
ISBN-10: 1935597515

To E.P., H.P., C.P.P., and John B. Breckinridge II

ONE

High noon over the Amazon. Tropical rainstorm skirting the Andes, greasing the alleys, and filling the cafes of cities far beyond the jungle.

Whitehill made no attempt to shield himself from the oncoming rain. He was already dripping with sweat.

Palms first, he lowered himself onto a section of fallen tree, stiffening his arms to take some of the weight off his legs. He closed his eyes and sighed like a man at his desk who realizes that the workload for the day is far more than he anticipated.

He remembered hearing somewhere that snakes make a habit of lying underneath logs, and he wearily shifted around to check behind.

No, no snakes. Whitehill dug his heels into the ground. He sat motionless as the storm broke overhead. It came in hard and fast, the drops gathering into thin channels, running off leaf to leaf. Whitehill moved his face under one of these, letting the tiny stream pass over his forehead, onto his tongue.

A dim internal signal of alarm alerted him that if the downpour continued it would turn the floor of the jungle

1

into mud, making his progress that much more difficult. Since this was beyond Whitehill's control, he ignored it. And that was when the first swell of panic caught in his throat.

For some time now, Whitehill had known he was lost. He was not the sort to respond coolly to matters of life and death, and when he realized he was viewing his own problem with such calm detachment, fear ripped through him.

The crush and tangle of green all around was becoming claustrophobic. He sat under seven or eight stories of canopy jungle. He had not had a clear look at the sun since hiking past the outskirts of town early that morning. Now it was probably afternoon. Twice he had imagined something large was stalking him.

Insects danced about his head, sang in his ear, explored his nose. Unseen birds and monkeys screeched and whistled his presence. A soiled, superfluous humidity tightened continually, holding the heat in close.

Life, all his thirty-one years of it, had not prepared Whitehill for any of this. He was a lawyer from Pittsburgh.

Within the first ten minutes on the trail, it had occurred to him that he might have ventured a little too far into the jungle. He had turned around immediately, but the narrow path he was following appeared much less distinct from this new perspective. Worse, there seemed to be three paths.

Nonetheless, Whitehill refused to believe he had become so turned around that he would be unable to find some way out. Shouting for help a kilometer or two from the streets of Lomalito had been unthinkable.

Now, clearly, that no longer mattered. Frustration and panic leapt out of him: "Heeeeeeeeey!" Clenching his fists, he straightened up, felt the softening ground yield under his feet, and sloshed around in a tight little circle. "Heey, anybody! Hello? Hey, help, hello!"

In anger, Whitehill grabbed a huge rubbery leaf and yanked down. It barely shuddered. He stared in disbelief and watched thick drops of rain disappear into his shirtsleeve.

This was the shirt he'd bought expressly for his trip, a quick-dry "expedition" shirt, "field-tested by globe-trotters," endorsed by mustachioed TV explorers, and, the salesman had stressed, fashionable as well. Whitehill swore under his breath. His choice of the Amazon had been directly connected with this purchase. People shouldn't be allowed to just wear these things. This whole predicament was somehow the shirt's fault.

Various ideas presented themselves to Whitehill's brain, which was in no condition to receive intruders. The opalescent light of the rain forest distorted his perception, straining his memory banks for parallels, operational cues. His last experience with the forces of nature had been the Colorado rafting trip he'd taken to impress his new secretary. He had returned home, toting eight boxes of slides, only to find she'd joined the Hare Krishnas in his absence.

It was now possible that he would have to spend the night in a jungle. Whitehill knew the importance of keeping his head, but many seconds passed before he could anchor his scrambled thoughts in the present.

Ryder or one of the others he had met at the cafe last night might ask after him, but that would not be until well after dark. Even so, he barely knew them and couldn't be sure they would miss him at all.

He had arrived in Lomalito only yesterday, had no business there, and no one expected him anywhere tonight.

Moreover, in a place like Lomalito people probably went off for days at a time with some regularity. How should he know?

Four weeks ago, a nascent adventurer, he'd begun a leave of absence from the law firm in which he was an associate. At the time, he had no intention of returning until he made his way around the world. To South America then (Europe he had conquered passably in eight weeks last summer), and Africa and Asia, however long it took. Looking down at the mud forming under his boots, he pondered the wisdom of this ambitious itinerary.

Whitehill was a good-natured fellow of medium height. His lean frame carried the first few extra pounds of middle age, although he looked much younger. The blond hair he had stopped trying to push off his forehead was never properly combed, giving him a relaxed, boyish appearance that made him attractive to young married women and elderly friends of the family.

Under his khaki shirt he wore the uniform of the young American traveler: colored T-shirt, jeans, and dark leather hiking boots with thick, waffled soles. Back in the biologist's paradise that passed for his hotel room, a down jacket was jammed into a bulging red backpack.

Except for the occasional chin-up or afternoon of tennis, Whitehill had had no real exercise since his entire high school baseball team had been suspended for trapping their coach in the locker room one weekend. He was tired, unprepared.

＊　＊　＊

During the last days of the conflict in Vietnam, Whitehill had finessed his way into an Air Force Reserve unit to avoid being drafted in the real army. One weekend a month for six years he had trimmed his hair, buttoned and zipped himself into uniform, and driven to Fort Green, where he filed medical records. His friends slept peacefully those years, knowing that if war were ever officially declared Whitehill would be manning his filing cabinet—zinging in folder after folder, papers flying, drawers slamming, both hands blurring with the acceleration the war effort demanded.

One thing was certain. If the Vietcong ever overran Pennsylvania, they would capture a set of medical records of which America could be proud. Each Smith filed right down to his middle initial, the Macs before the Mcs, the Cohns cross-referenced with the Cohens.

On those days when the military was on without-Whitehill status, he practiced his impersonation of an attorney. He took all the courses, received and framed the necessary degrees, and passed several state bar examinations, but his heart was never in it. Whitehill had been among the legion of college seniors who sense that they are about to be popped into the existential void. One sleepless night they imagine themselves flapping about the streets with no clothes, no direction, no identity, and in the morning they write off for law school applications.

Those law school years were difficult for Whitehill. He was forever stumbling through hallways, bouncing around the libraries, knocking into classmates, ranting, "What am I doing here? What's it all about? Where am I? What's happening? Where are we going?"

Classmate: Good morning, Whitehill.

Whitehill: You know, life is strange…

His friends were fond of him and treated him like a beloved relation turned eccentric in his later years. Whitehill was universally regarded as an endangered species that had somehow been captured in Pittsburgh.

Over these last six years he had practiced law and promised himself a long vacation when his hitch in the reserves was over. Then, he had given up his apartment, stored his clothes in his parents' attic, downed a few tequilas with his law partners, smoked a last joint with his old college roommates, said good-bye to his girlfriend, Monica, who had maintained for months that the trip would be beneficial for their relationship, spent his last Pittsburgh evening in her bed, was thrown out of her apartment at four in the morning ("You don't really care about me!"), walked three miles for a taxi, and landed much later that night in Bogotá.

Whitehill toured the museums, photographed the monuments, and visited the cathedrals. He took planes, trains, and buses. He learned that everyone in Ecuador is five feet tall, that coca leaves in Peru are not chewed like spinach, that Colombia is more famous for its thieves than its pre-Columbian art, and that Bolivians eat a lot of potatoes.

He had a fleeting exchange of passion in a darkened hotel corridor with a Jewish girl from Miami trying to pass herself off as a street-hardened drug dealer. She wore no underwear. He unzipped his pants. She raised bare suntanned legs up out of her dress and pulled her knees behind his shoulders. He grabbed her wrists, stretching out her arms to the point of pain.

They arched into each other. At the moment of elation, she laced her legs around him, threw back her head, and screamed, "Oy! Oy! Oy! Oy! Oy!" Whitehill paid without hesitation when the hotel manager charged him double the next morning. There was little about his trip that was exotic or even stimulating. Most of his advance reservations had been changed, canceled, or delayed. He was disappointed, slipping into depression. There was no place he wished to go that he would just as soon not go.

He watched barefoot peasants sleeping in doorways, urinating on the main streets of capital cities, staring up at skyscrapers. An idea for an essay on frailty began to take shape in his head. He started following albinos, dwarves, and cripples through the city streets, jotting down his thoughts in a small notebook.

Crossing at a busy intersection one afternoon, Whitehill dropped his little notebook. His thoughts were in the clouds, common enough for Whitehill, but not recommended procedure for challenging the brand of driver found south of the border. A late-model Chevrolet clipped him from behind as he bent over, somersaulting the essayist onto his back.

Somewhat dazed, he staggered back to his hotel, where the elderly hotelkeeper and her newly married daughter put him to bed. They brought him a pot of hot tea, a two-week-old copy of the *International Herald Tribune*, and a South American guidebook rescued from the hotel trash bin.

The tea was unusually bitter, but it seemed to make him more alert, and he began to take an interest in the travel book. He was not unrewarded.

Lomalito—something of an oddity among jungle towns, this charming little Amazon riverport is built around the base of a small hill, from which it takes its name. There are plans to open an airport at the end of this year (a quick check of the front cover revealed the book to be four years old) *and tourist-class hotels cannot be far behind. Animal life abounds, and the heartier traveler can engage a guide and set off into the jungle on his own.*

It had never occurred to Whitehill that such a thing was possible. He had always imagined that a party of porters and gun bearers worthy of a Tarzan movie would be needed for any kind of excursion into the jungle. Apparently this town was off the beaten track, yet accessible now by plane. More importantly, one could travel through the jungle from there without joining a tour group, contrary to what travel agents in the States had told him.

The next morning he was on a bus to El Trabajoso, where it would be possible to book a flight into Lomalito. He was delayed en route due to a small landslide, arriving two hours past Aero Amazonia's scheduled departure time. It took him another hour to locate the ticket office, which proved to be the produce counter of the local grocery, but the clerk assured Whitehill that he had arrived in plenty of time.

The traveler had just settled down behind two mottled bananas and a lukewarm Inca Cola when an Aero Amazonia passenger bus pulled up, the same one he had just gotten off, now sporting a freshly painted green-and-white "Aeropuerto" sign taped inside the windshield.

On the trip in to El Trabajoso, he had been jammed between a *mestizo* holding an armful of chickens and a tuberculous old woman who drooled and spit continually into a tin cup. Now he was the only passenger.

The driver was a short, thick man with olive brown features. He turned in his seat, rubbed his fingers through greasy black hair, and shook hands with Whitehill. "OK. OK. We go. You got cigarette?" The clerk came out from behind the counter with a fifty-kilo bag of rice, climbed on the bus, and dumped it in the aisle. For the first time, Whitehill noticed a machete on his hip. There was some peculiar disease crawling up his ankles, which probably wasn't helped by the fact that the clerk obviously never wore shoes. The skin over his feet looked like petrified bread, a sharp contrast to the smooth, oily skin stretched over the muscles in his arm. Sizing up the clerk's patched brown pants and torn "American League Beisbol" T-shirt, Whitehill knew this was not a fellow he would easily forget.

The bus engine complained, stuttered, and then started. Reaching behind the visor, the driver pulled out a dusty pilot's cap with the Aero Amazonia logo. He fumbled under his seat, produced a slightly less elegant version of the same cap, flipped it to the clerk, who slid into the seat next to Whitehill, and they were off.

The afternoon heat pushed Whitehill to the point of irritation as the bus slowly and protestingly snaked its way out of El Trabajoso. In the next seat, the clerk used both hands on the brim of his cap to bend it properly over his brow. He bucked and nodded in his excitement, chanting, "*Aeropuerto, aeropuerto.*"

El Trabajoso was not very large. It took only a few minutes to round the main plaza, negotiate a labyrinth of dirt streets, and head into the countryside. After three or four kilometers, the bus turned at what looked like a huge, abandoned scrap-metal yard. Whitehill had seen no "Aeropuerto" signs.

As they drove between mounds of rusting junk, Whitehill made out a clearing just ahead. The bus was heading right for the clearing, which had incredibly revealed itself to be a large body of water. There were no airplanes, no other cars, and no people. Whitehill found himself stiffening.

He watched with horror as the clerk crossed his leg, brushing one of those impossible feet over Whitehill's hand. They drew up to a long pier, and the driver turned in. It was a dead end with water on all sides. They drove straight to the far edge.

Without so much as a glance back at Whitehill, the clerk and the driver got out and walked to an old wooden rowboat. They bent over its greasy outboard motor, coaxed the thing to life, and shouted at Whitehill, "*Aeropuerto, aeropuerto.*"

Whitehill grabbed his backpack, had a fleeting vision of a small Pennsylvania farmhouse on a snow-covered hill, smoke curling out of the chimney at sundown, and then jumped off the bus. He stepped into a center seat in the boat, a barely floating, well-past-its-prime construction of raw, rotting wood bleached gray-brown where it was dry.

They roared off running crosswise to the current. After a short time, waves lapped into the boat, soaking Whitehill from the waist down. He quickly learned to anticipate them and twist out of their way

Pointing at the opposite shore, his two companions began to shout "Aeropuerto" again. All Whitehill could make out was a sharp rise of thick green growth. A jagged string of copper-brown path ran up the middle, breaking the center point of the horizon in two, like locked pieces of some god's jigsaw puzzle carelessly pushed off a celestial table, now fallen to earth.

It was fast upon them. The boat slipped softly into the shore mud. Half a dozen earth-colored children in tattered shorts materialized out of the bush, grabbing for Whitehill's backpack.

"*No, no, tengo, gracias.*"

The clerk lifted his sack of rice out of the boat, lined up three of the larger children, and dropped it on their heads. Whitehill imagined their fragile spines jamming into sunsoftened brains at the base of still-forming skulls. Losing their collective balance under the first impact, they steadied themselves in a moment, never taking their eyes off Whitehill.

The driver yelled to the clerk to push the boat off, then to Whitehill, "*Adios, señor, bye-bye, buen viaje!*"

Whitehill waved a beat or two and began to climb the path. With the boat's departure, he gave himself up to his situation. He would have chosen to be last in line, but the children were so interested in watching him that he wound up first.

There was donkey shit to be avoided at every step. Of necessity Whitehill watched the path sliding under him, walking faster than he might have had he not been in the lead. Reaching the summit, he noticed for the first time what he hoped was a control tower, a two-story, tin-and-cinder-block structure perhaps a thousand yards off. It became enormously important to Whitehill that things should go more or less as planned. Since his accident, he was no longer as willing to find charm in Latin inefficiency.

He marched his group in, children following closely, the clerk adjusting his hat at the rear.

Two counters faced across the room. One bore the Aero Amazonia logo, the other, a cardboard sign of two clinking champagne glasses with ascending bubbles.

A surprisingly beautiful girl flipped through a stack of paper at Aero Amazonia while two couples drank and joked across the way. Whitehill guessed they were newly met by the flirtatious charge in the air.

He checked in with the beautiful young lady and thought about falling in love, about making love to a woman from another culture, about living in that other culture.

She smiled. He thought of many things to say and said none of them.

"*Equipaje, señor?*" asked the clerk with a servile bow.

Whitehill surrendered the bulging red backpack as the sound of an airplane filled the room. It emerged from behind giant trees and bounced down in a puff of dust at the far end of a clearing cut from the forest.

Pounding up to the terminal, the pilot stopped into a quick ninety-degree turn. He threw a cloth shoulder bag out of the plane and leaped drunkenly after it, falling in the dust.

He got up shakily, only to be tackled again by the two men who had been drinking at the bar. This time, laughing, they all had trouble standing up.

Whitehill could not help noticing that all three men wore identical clothing: Aero Amazonia uniforms.

Twenty minutes later, they were airborne. The incoming pilot had been induced to make the return trip and was passed out in the last of six rows of seats. The beautiful girl was now the stewardess, but Whitehill barely noticed because the two men he had seen drinking at the bar were, of course, the new pilots. Each was flying with one of the women on his lap.

Cargo was tied down the length of the aisle, squeezed under the seats and lashed over them: chickens roped together at the legs; huge bags of noodles, rice, and flour; filthy crates from CARE; mysterious sacks and cans "donated by the people of the United States."

Whitehill again was the only passenger. He looked out over the horizon, then down at his shirt, focusing on one after another of the little dirt specks settling there. The plane had been descending since takeoff. Apparently the airport was on some deceptively high plateau. The forest beneath grew tighter. But for the soft, curving brown rivers glinting silver below, it was impossible to see anything but leaves. Even in these last minutes of daylight, the jungle was quite literally steaming.

The plane banked into the sunset over Lomalito, a red-orange sun bleeding into low-lying clouds as it dropped into the jungle, all on a backdrop of deep cobalt blue. But what occupied Whitehill most were the concerns of the traveler.

Will there be a taxi? What might be the going rate into town? Can these jokers actually land this plane? How will I find a hotel, centrally located? Did they load my bag?

The landing was unexpectedly uneventful.

Whitehill gave himself up to the only taxi at the airstrip, bargaining so as not to appear an easy mark. They drove across the runway, which doubled as part of some local avenue.

There was a one-lane wooden bridge, a row of grass huts, a red-and-white-striped barricade manned by two soldiers in different uniforms, who raised it by both sitting on one end, seesaw style, and then Lomalito. His driver steered him to a place called the Cafe Hotel. Lomalito appeared so small there seemed no need to ask if he was in the center of town.

It was certain that the driver would receive a commission for bringing in a new guest. Whitehill knew this would inflate his own rate, but the hotel owner was a sleazy, hard-sell type and Whitehill was still off balance in a new environment, so he did what was easiest.

Minutes after checking in, there was a knock on his door. "*Señor*, you have American dollars?" asked the hotel owner, a sharp tongue probing brown cracks in his smile.

"I have a few," Whitehill returned cautiously.

"My name John."

"Juan?"

"No, John."

"John?"

"*Sí*, anything you need, ask Señor John. You want boat trip. You want guide. You want girls. You want fishing. Ask Señor John. You can pay me American dollars, I give free breakfast."

"What's for breakfast?"

"Oh breakfast, oh very good, oh boy." Señor John slowly ticked off the menu on his fingers, "Oh, we give toast, tea, coffee, biscuits, butter, margarine, jelly..."

"Señor John, that's bread and water."

Señor John pondered that for a moment and seemed quite pleased when he got the joke; he was not pleased so much by the humor but by the fact that he had gotten away with charging high prices for commodities that were even less valuable than he had considered.

He stood in the doorway and looked off toward the ceiling, appearing to forget all about Whitehill as he calculated his margin of profit with a new sense of understanding. Whitehill, for his part, reasoned that if Señor John could find a more rewarding exchange rate for dollars than the one given at the bank, so could he.

Whitehill ran both hands through his pockets, reassuring himself that his money was still there, bills in the front (more difficult for pickpockets), coins buttoned into his shirt, traveler's checks in his left boot, passport in his right.

He left Señor John to his thoughts, edging them both gently out of the room as he closed the door.

The one-floor Cafe Hotel was a squat, cream-colored building with rounded arches and softened corners. At the end of a spacious central hallway, two ceiling fans pushed the thick evening air down toward a plastic bust of John Kennedy. Whitehill placed his room key on a board of numbered hooks in the lobby and walked out into the night.

"OK, OK," called Señor John after him, "no breakfast."

Whitehill found himself at the center of a circle of light under the hotel street lamp, one of perhaps a dozen in town. A cloud of insects spun overhead. The Cafe Hotel faced a wide dirt alley opposite the tiny brick Hotel Residencia and a smaller wooden shack called Siete Chicas Bar. The name was painted on the door in alternating psychedelic colors laid over a picture of two clinking beer bottles. Jungle was on his right, Lomalito's main intersection to his left.

Something in that direction made him flinch. Stepping over slowly to the fuzzy edge of brightness, Whitehill could make out the flattened remains of a large snake, dried into the mud by an equatorial sun.

At that moment, all light disappeared. He looked up quickly to get a visual bearing for balance. It occurred to him that the snake at his feet might not be dead—he had seen it for only a second—but the rush of blackness had caught Whitehill so completely off guard he couldn't be sure which way he was facing.

There was little moon and less sky than Whitehill could ever remember. It was all stars. Psychodynamic relays clicked inside him, calculating the new numbers and spatial relations of the heavens in this strange hemisphere.

The apparent power failure pointed up what a fragile position Lomalito was in, hanging at the edge of the world's most powerful river in the middle of an untamed rain forest. Inaccessible by road, all supplies shipped or flown in, the town was able to make only a tentative stand for civilization. Whitehill shivered involuntarily. But for tufts of weeds sprouting in sidewalk cracks, he had never known land that resisted. Rolling his head back, he followed the sweep of stars around him until he picked out the line of treetops. A spoke of flame to his right, a candle placed in the window of Siete Chicas. The press of black jungle against one yellow-white light reflecting a wooden window frame, a patch of dirt street.

Cheers went up as a staccato series of flashes announced the imminent return of electricity. More lights blinked on around him. The snake was dead and obviously of little interest to anyone around here. Patterns of tire treads ran broadly across its back; mud caked in the folds under its eyes.

Whitehill was surprised to discover he had an erection.

He felt a primal chord had been struck, one somehow resonant with fear, but he could make no sense of it. Surveying the mud streets, he wondered if perhaps he understood something of the jungle. At bottom, he knew he was only a kid from the suburbs who'd just seen a dead snake, but he was in the Amazon now beyond any question. Whitehill let that thought hook into him, and it pulled him, grinning, toward the Siete Chicas bar.

The door stood slightly ajar, and Whitehill slipped through quietly to avoid attracting attention. Though quite pleased with his growing capacity for boldness, Whitehill realized that he knew nothing of such places. A small part of him stood ready to receive beer bottles over the head.

16

"*Hola, hombre!*"

"*Buenas noches.*" After ordering a scotch with ice cream in a hotel bar the previous week, Whitehill was not eager to test his command of Spanish much further. But it was one of those situations from which a speedy, graceful retreat was not possible. There were only four men in the room, each looking straight at him, no empty chairs.

The interior of Siete Chicas was roughly the size and had the feel of an old wooden boxcar. A counter cut midway across its width, blocking patrons' access to a few grimy stacks of canned goods and an aging German refrigerator that hung halfway out the back door, whirring and coughing into the night.

"*Cerveza, señor?*" This from a thin, smiling man in beard and beret. Half naked and deeply tanned, he stood hunched behind the counter.

"No, Bernardo! Wait a minute. Give this guy some *chuchuasco.*"

Whitehill processed the suggestion as a friendly challenge, coming as it did from a young, bearded American whose eyes betrayed any attempt the rest of his features might make at expressions other than happiness. He was balanced almost impossibly on a low wooden stool, feet up on the counter, one shoulder against the wall, half twisting backward to size up the stranger. Flanking him on one side was a broad, silver-haired, European-looking fellow who watched Whitehill over the rim of his glass, and on the other, a fat man overflowing the only object in the room that reasonably passed as a chair.

"Sit down, pal. We're all drinking it," said the fat man. "Great stuff. If you ever find a clean woman in this town, it'll

17

make you fuck like hell. And if you can't find one, *chuchuasco* will make you forget all about it."

"Sure," returned Whitehill, cautiously eying a large, muscular spider crawling laterally across Bernardo's refrigerator. "What is it?"

"We don't really know," laughed the American. "Bernardo here is something of a *brujo*, a sorcerer. He pulls a couple of roots out of the jungle, marinates them in grain alcohol and *aguardiente*, and there it is."

A chuckling Bernardo grabbed two evil-looking bottles from the bottom shelf of his refrigerator and poured equal portions of each into four glasses already lined up on the counter.

The fat man raised his to eye level. "What's your name?"

"Whitehill."

"Well, Whitehill, old pal, when you spend any time in this part of the world, you're always looking for a little patch of shade. This here's it."

"I'm Ryder," offered the American. "The gentleman doing all the drinking and talking, and usually all the eating, is Señor McJeffers; and from the shores of Bahia, most recently returned from the African continent, Mr. Rudolph Boas."

The man called Boas passed a glass to Whitehill. "I believe, Señor Whitehill, that you will find this spot most agreeable," he said, motioning to a clean bit of floor opposite a side entrance. "It's best not to go for too much altitude at first."

Whitehill propped himself tailor fashion against the wall and tested his *chuchuasco*. It was strong and hard, but he was relieved to find he could get it down.

Courting approval, he swallowed rapidly and held out his glass for a refill. It did not escape Whitehill's attention that the view through the side entrance was his first of the

Amazon River. Gentle waves lapped softly into river mud outside the door. A lone cooking fire flickered miles away on the opposite bank.

"Hey, Whitehill, what are you doing down here?" asked McJeffers.

Whitehill looked up in surprise.

"No, I don't mean down on the floor. I mean Lomalito."

"Tourist?" ventured Boas.

"I guess that is what I am. You don't get many tourists?" Whitehill was a little worried about losing the exclusivity of his accomplishment. He had already resolved to consecrate this evening by sticking a finger in the water on the way back to his hotel.

McJeffers threw down another *chuchuasco*. "Had one just last week, a great one, a hippie." He laughed, shifted his chair, and began to settle into the evening.

Rings of sweat widened under the arms of all as Bernardo automatically topped off the glasses.

"This guy was truly wonderful," McJeffers went on. "He shows up in town one day 'looking for adventure.' I swear to Christ that's what he said. The first damn afternoon he's here, a little fer-de-lance went for him from behind and caught his fangs in the guy's bell-bottom pants. He must've dragged the thing twenty feet before he felt it. Fainted dead away. Ha ha. What a damn jerk."

"How big is a little fer-de-lance?" asked Whitehill.

"Don't worry, man," said Ryder. "You almost never run into snakes in town. Too much action for them to hang around."

"Glad to hear that," Whitehill returned, thinking that he'd already seen one, but holding himself back from asking, "How often is 'almost never'?"

"May I ask, Señor Whitehill, where you have chosen to reside in this elegant metropolis of ours?" asked Boas.

"I just checked into the Cafe Hotel."

"Ha! Señor John's place. What a fuckin' crook," laughed McJeffers between gulps.

"Yeah, I'd watch out for him," offered Ryder, who by now had taken possession of Bernardo's bottles.

"How come?"

"Because," Boas said, "Señor John feels that his only mission in life is to somehow transfer any money you have from your pockets into his."

"A fuckin' crook."

Ryder smiled, watching McJeffers's chuckle explode into a rapid rumble of choking coughs, *chuchuasco* shooting out his nose. The vibrations sent dangerous squeaks through the hinges of his chair. "Just let Señor John know that you're onto him and you'll be OK," said Ryder.

McJeffers, struggling now to gain control of a wheezing, breathless laugh that threatened the future existence of Siete Chicas, managed to squeeze out, "Don't take the jungle tour."

He was joined enthusiastically by Whitehill who, having lost count of *chuchuascos*, was just sane enough to ask, "What am I laughing about?"

"Señor John keeps a couple of Yaguas on retainer," explained Ryder. "He gets 'em to hide in the bush with a blowgun so his hotel guests can just 'happen' upon them 'hunting' at the end of his 'Amazon tour.' Mostly, they all go for it."

"Ha ha ha, what's a Yagua?"

"The Yaguas are the legendary Amazons," said Boas, examining the refractions of Bernardo's lone electric light bulb in his glass.

"Yeah," Ryder picked up, "they've always worn what look like grass skirts. That's why the old Spaniards thought they were fighting women warriors. They're kind of candy-ass now."

"Huh, I never knew that," said Whitehill.

"Oh yeah, they're candy-ass all right. Takes ten off 'em to kill a monkey," said McJeffers.

"No, I mean I never knew about where Amazons came from."

"Um, true story," Ryder continued. "Anyway, the tourist thing never made it too big down here. Lomalito's still pretty much a backwater. You never know, though, with all that 'adventure travel' business back in the States. Jesus, you two probably don't know about that, do you? All you've got to do now is send away for a color brochure and sign on the dotted line. Then you just show up at the airport where some guy takes you by the hand and eventually leads you up a mountain or down a river and you sit between a dentist from Long Island and a college kid from Los Angeles and pretend you're having an adventure."

"No shit?" exclaimed McJeffers.

"Is there any dirt involved?" asked Boas.

"Well, I think they'd ask for their money back if there wasn't any dirt," Ryder returned.

"Now hold on a second. What's wrong with people wanting to experience something new?" Whitehill asked.

"Nothing," said Ryder. "There are just too many of them. The land can't handle it."

"Oh no. Whitehill, don't get him started," McJeffers pleaded.

"Somehow, the wilderness got to be hip. TV burnout, probably, pushing everybody outside. What you've got now are all these Californians trading in their gurus for backpacks. They camp a place to death. Bathe in water the wildlife needs, bury garbage the animals will only dig up, wear those lug-soled shoes that tear up the ground cover...and these are the enlightened ones."

Ryder filled his glass, emptied it, and filled another.

"If it's any small satisfaction to you, Señor Ryder," said Boas, "consider that the owners of these travel agencies will find that there are no longer any quiet paradises to retire to with the fortunes they've made promoting them."

"Ha ha ha, thank you, Boas. That will be a great comfort to me when I'm caught in a canoe traffic jam or waiting for a signal light on the trail."

"Hey, Whitehill, you're not scouting for adventure travelers, are ya?" McJeffers asked.

"No no, just passing through. What do you guys do?"

"Mainly this," laughed Ryder, raising a bottle slightly. "Tell you what though, Whitehill. If you want some help or information or anything, you can probably find us here tomorrow night. Me for sure, I think. You definitely did the right thing coming here. The jungle's fucking great."

"Thanks, I appreciate that." Whitehill stared through his glass into the light. "I might check things out on my own a little before then."

"Señor Whitehill."

"Yes, Señor Boas?"

"If you are thinking of taking a small hike, I suggest sunrise."

"Early morning and late afternoon are the only times anybody moves around down here," Ryder explained. "Jungle's pretty in the morning, but don't underestimate it."

McJeffers looked up from behind his *chuchuasco.* "Boy, that's damn right. You can get turned around pretty fuckin' easy."

Ryder stood. "Well, I'm going to hit it, let Bernardo grab a little peace. Leave a big tip, will ya, McJeffers? I don't want you embarrassing me."

TWO

Whitehill walked without rhythm, sometimes catching his foot on a trailing vine, sometimes unexpectedly stepping on a small rise. The underbrush was dense and irregular, as high as his chest, never much below his knees. It was impossible to see where he placed his feet.

Green leaves, snags, branches, and huge, low-lying roots assailed him on all sides. Each step was somehow difficult. Whitehill reached into his pocket and pulled out the Swiss Army knife he had bought at a hardware store in Quito. It had a corkscrew, scissors, bottle opener, can opener, two blades, a miniature saw, tweezers, toothpick, and a little cross for warding off vampires.

He selected the longest blade. There was no lock on the knife. He would have to remember to slash outward so as not to close it on his fingers. Whitehill held the knife up against the last, fading moments of daylight, smiled for a moment, and then let his arm fall. The Swiss Army knife was one of the smallest things in the jungle.

Whitehill felt the heat push him back against a tree. He was running out of time. The quality of the jungle was shifting; colors and noises were deepening.

There was nothing to do now but run. He had been all day without food and, worse, with little water. The *chuchuasco* stretched up his throat. Whitehill wanted to vomit, but he caught himself and swallowed.

It was as though he had swallowed adrenaline. He ran faster. His legs seemed disconnected from his body. Whitehill lost track of time and caution. He only knew he had to move as fast as possible.

He crashed through the jungle like a fullback, imagining the animals of the night fleeing before him, then doubling back behind to check out this strange creature. Every few steps, he stumbled, pulled himself up, and ran again.

Branches grabbed at his hair, caught his shirt. His face was torn.

Whitehill slashed into a smother of leaves, but they held, and he could not break through. He twisted violently, pushing with his legs. Straining at the vines wrapping tightly around his chest, he spun free and fell heavily into a ditch.

He turned onto his back, propped himself up on his elbows. Whitehill looked up at the moon. He was lying in a clearing slicing through the jungle. Another ditch ran parallel to his own. Tire tracks.

This was great. Probably the greatest moment of his life. So he wasn't going to die after all. He need only follow the tire tracks. One way certainly had to lead back to Lomalito, but the other direction also had to lead somewhere. Either way, he was saved.

Instantly, his sense of reason returned, followed closely by his sense of humor. Whitehill laughed out loud. He stood up slowly and felt around the places that hurt. There were a number of cuts on his hands and face, some of them deep and already swelling. His shirt was ripped. Blood stained from underneath and dried into the tear.

The sounds of the jungle edged their way back into his thoughts. Shrieks that he guessed must be howler monkeys and, underneath that, the unrelenting buzz of insects. McJeffers had said something about vampire bats that prowled at night. Rolling swarms of vampire bats, sucking blood through their tubelike tongues. Jesus, he was not out of this yet. In fact, he was still profoundly scared. At any moment a jaguar could leap on him from behind, or why not from in front? Big difference. There wasn't much light; he could easily step on a snake. A spider would be bad enough. Anything.

Now, which way was Lomalito? Impossible to know. Left seemed to be right. To the left then.

The going was easier here, but still the undergrowth slowed his progress. Whitehill watched his feet. From time to time he checked over a shoulder. Every shadow was threatening. Every sound hurried him ahead.

Whitehill puffed up his chest, pulled back his shoulders, and threw out his arms—all to make himself appear as big as possible. "I must look like fuckin' Frankenstein. That's all right though, that's all right. Nobody messes with Frankenstein. Frankenstein is bad news, man. Fuck with Frankenstein, you see how bad he is…I'm going crazy here."

He pulled out the knife, testing the blades with his thumb. "What the hell do the Swiss know about the fucking jungle? They live in the Alps, they're all goddamn bankers, and they never fight anywhere. That's why I'm lost in the goddamn Amazon fucking jungle and I've got to defend myself with a corkscrew. Way to go, Whitehill. Great choice of weapons."

It was his only weapon though, and the only thing he had to hold on to. A stick would work well in his other hand, kind of balance out his attack nicely. The thick one under those leaves seemed right. He bent for it, but other muscles inside him, stronger ones, cried out, "Snake!"

Whitehill screamed. Even as he began to run, he knew it had not been a snake. It hadn't looked anything like a snake. But the possibility of snake was enough, and running was all his body would allow him.

Whitehill fled deeper into the night. He was breathing hard and attending only to that sound. His lungs throbbed, the tendons in his legs throbbed, his thoughts throbbed. "Shit."

He slowed down, hands on hips to ease the pain in his chest. Shorter steps. The air, thick and moist, was on him more than around him. He gulped at it, and the air, too, seemed to resist him.

Whitehill imagined a glow buried in the leaves. And then voices. Two voices, growing louder. This was it. Wasn't it? He rushed ahead. Not English. Not any language he'd ever heard, almost a singsong, Oriental sound. He stopped.

No reason to fear that. We're not at war with anybody. Maybe there are a lot of bandits around. Hell, so what, they can have the Swiss Army knife. Can't just run in there, but if I sneak around, that'll seem suspicious. Somewhere in the middle I guess, just come right in, slowly.

A small shack waited for him in the trees, most of an old Land Rover parked to one side. Rich orange light poured from behind, making it difficult to pick out any detail. The voices were clear now, and too loud. Unsettling, like two cats arguing.

Not inviting, but the only choice available. He walked around back.

Three grown men shrieked at once, Whitehill one of them. An older, bearded man fell to the ground. Whitehill was not even sure the other was human. Barely five feet tall, naked but for some strips of color, a roll of leaf between the legs, and thick, pulsing shadows painted on by the fire. Yet human enough to have a bow and arrow leveled at Whitehill's chest.

"Friend!" Whitehill reached for the stars. "Hold it. Hold it. Wait. Friend…friend…shit…easy…*amigo?* Friend? Lomalito, OK? *Amigo*…friend."

The older man stood. "Where the hell did you come from?"

"God, you speak English."

"Yes, what are you doing here?"

"My name's Whitehill. I'm staying in Lomalito. Got lost."

"Lomalito's almost ten kilometers from here."

"I've been lost all day. Could you ask him to please point that away from me?"

"I see."

It seemed to Whitehill that his request was considered a shade too long. He desperately wanted to behave like something more than a hysterical jerk, but it was only after the little man heard the other say "*Bakiratare, ka*," and relaxed the bowstring that Whitehill began to compose himself. After all, they had been equally frightened. Considering that he'd just had a six-foot arrow aimed at his heart, Whitehill assured himself that he had acted rather favorably. Pretty damn cool.

"You may put your hands down now if you like."

"Oh, right."

The little man, the Indian, walked up to Whitehill and stopped less than a foot away. They regarded each other a moment, and then the Indian pulled Whitehill's shirt out of his pants and began to examine the stitching.

"Please relax, Mr. Whitehall. I assure you this is quite normal."

"White*hill*."

"Excuse me."

The Indian had quickly worked his way around front and was massaging the buttons of Whitehill's shirt between his fingers. He smelled like an old piece of cheese left too long in the afternoon sun.

"How long will this last?"

"That will probably depend on how tired he is. If you wish to speed things up, empty your pockets."

"What?"

"Nothing will be stolen, although it may be a while before your things are returned."

Whitehill obediently went through his pockets, hampered a bit by the Indian, who was unsuccessfully trying to remove his belt. He held back his passport and traveler's checks, producing a little money, his knife, a vitamin pill, and a receipt from the Cafe Hotel. The Indian brought them near the fire and seemed not to notice when the receipt was plucked from his hand.

"Hmm. Señor John. He overcharged you."

This was no surprise and of little importance to White-hill. He had begun to realize that he was having a normal conversation and was thankful. "Do you have something to drink?"

"Yes, of course. I apologize. You must be thirsty. How did you manage to get lost?"

"It wasn't hard. Just decided to take a walk in the jungle. Got mixed up. For hours now I've been thinking I'd never get out."

"Yes." He looked closely at Whitehill and then turned and walked back to the fire, squatting next to the Indian so that their shoulders touched.

In the uneven light, Whitehill judged the fellow to be about fifty, slight of build, with eyes and nose too large for his face. The Indian was solid, perhaps no more than twenty. He had a mane of dark hair and wide, flat hands and feet. The two spoke quietly.

"Listen, I don't want to…uh, can I have that drink?"

"Yes, yes, I'd forgotten. Please excuse me. Here, come on in."

They left the Indian alone. Whitehill caught a last glimpse of him at the fire, blowing his nose into a bill of large denomination.

Once inside, Whitehill's companion lit an oil lamp and fussed with various objects in a shadowy corner of the shack's only room. Valiant attempts had been made here to deny the presence of the jungle outside, but in vain. Humidity had invaded the cushions on a set of Italian easy chairs, lumping the stuffing and pulling life from the springs. The veneer of a large desk jammed flush against one wall curled and bubbled at the corners. The papers spread over its surface were splotched brown and stuck together.

A large map of the region, straining at its thumbtacks, hung tentatively over a sparsely stocked field bar. Across the room, impressively framed paintings leaned atop stacks of new wooden crates. Gray film spread over the surface of each, disguising the artists' intentions.

Whitehill's host stepped softly around piles of empty boxes and cans of food pushed to the edges of a worn oriental rug. He handed Whitehill a beer. "Not too cold, I'm afraid."

"Oh, it'll be great."

"I'm Dr. Darreiro."

"How do you do?"

Dr. Darreiro produced a small radio-cassette player and snapped in a tape. The soundtrack to *Doctor Zhivago*. He spun the bass and balance knobs to his satisfaction and then walked to the windows, inspecting mosquito nets cut and stretched to hold out the night. There was no breeze.

Whitehill attacked his bottle of beer, splashing a bit out of the corners of his mouth onto the shoulders of his already well-moistened shirt. He grinned foolishly and tried to assume the obvious postures of a guest who hasn't had enough.

"So, Mr. Whitehill, what are you doing here?"

Whitehill told him the story of his life, adding a few observations about life in general where appropriate. The beer had made him content and expansive, and he spoke rapidly, in a single rush. Fatigue and thirst caught him again as his narrative reached the ordeal of that very afternoon.

"It must be wonderful to pick up and leave like that," said Dr. Darreiro. "Wander at will."

"Didn't seem so great today, but yeah."

"And you have no itinerary? No one knows where you are?"

"That was kind of the idea. People send mail ahead to American Express, but all anyone knows is that I'm generally making my way south. So, if they get a postcard from, say, Quito, they write me in Lima. Or maybe La Paz to play it safe... May I have another beer? I know you have to haul all this stuff out here, but when I get back to Lomalito..."

"No problem, Mr. Whitehall. I wonder why Lomalito though? Do you have friends there?"

"It's White*hill*. No, I don't know a soul. Just picked it out of a book."

"Very adventurous of you. But I guess that is the kind of thing you can do when you have no appointments, not expected anywhere. You just follow your whims."

"I know. It's terrific. And it always pays off in unexpected ways. Like, I think I'll always remember this beer as the best I ever drank."

"Ah, well, let me get another for you to evaluate. You might want a glass of water first. You've been through a lot, and there is no sense assaulting your system."

Dr. Darreiro rose and was out the door with a speed of which Whitehill would not have thought him capable. He was a few minutes talking with his Indian friend, then returned with a glass of water in one hand and Whitehill's possessions in the other.

"Thank you. You know, Dr. Darreiro, I realize I've been talking so much I haven't given you a chance to say anything. What brought you to this place?"

"Here, finish that, and I'll pour you a beer. OK? Me? Oh, I'm one of those eccentric professors on sabbatical."

"Where do you teach?"

"I'm not teaching anywhere now. This is research for me. Why, within a hundred-yard radius of where we sit there are at least a dozen species of plants and insects that have never been cataloged. Perhaps a bird or snake as well..."

Whitehill listened with interest. It struck him that Dr. Darreiro might be the smartest man he'd ever met. A kind man, too, and generous. That was strange. Whitehill could remember vaguely disliking the guy.

He told Whitehill the most remarkable things, and they seemed to fit in perfectly with this room of his. This would be a great place to live. The heat wasn't so bad. Kind of comforting, somehow. It made the room larger. Maybe he would stay here awhile, help Dr. Darreiro with his research, get to know that Indian. Dr. Darreiro was saying something about the Indians. That he grew Indians maybe. No, that couldn't be right. Injuns. That's what they used to call them on Saturday morning television. Ha! Injun trouble. And he almost got shot by an Injun tonight. ("Whatever happened to Whitehill?" "Oh, he got shot with an arrow. Injun killed him.")

Whitehill dropped his glass and watched the beer foam dance on the rug. Didn't sound like the glass broke. Well, can't get the beer back in anyhow. He could scratch his nose now that his hand was free. He looked up at Dr. Darreiro but could not focus.

"Oh no." Whitehill pulled himself out of the chair and aimed for the door. He banged both hands against it, pushing into the blackness. The stars were above. They turned into comets as he collapsed.

* * *

In the dream Whitehill drove an old car, lactescent white with rolled and pleated white leather inside. He slowed for a young woman, browned and burned by the sun. She slipped softly into the rear seat, removed a dress. Perspiration beaded over the muscles of her stomach, trickled inside strong thighs. Whitehill watched as she fell back, letting her legs play smoothly against each other, toes probing warm folds in the leather. He wondered what mark a body might leave, if something of her would remain. Whitehill locked his hands in the moistness beneath the woman and floated on top. He pulled down into her, but he was alone.

THREE

It was cooler now. No, not cooler, a stirring in the air. Whitehill could not move at first. He felt himself being rocked
slightly and opened his eyes.

The sun ran through the leaves high overhead. Whitehill
was passing underneath, sliding silently, flat on his back. Someone moved in front, paddling, sitting on a red backpack—his.
Whitehill tried to get up.

"Yeaaa!"

"Idiot! Sit down. You'll turn us over."

That seemed like the right idea. Laughter from behind.
The Indian. Whitehill was in a dugout canoe, and he con-
gratulated himself briefly for recognizing it as such.

Dr. Darreiro turned. "*Bakiratare, ki-asateya.*"

"Hey, what's going on here?"

"Please be quiet. I'll explain later."

"Are we headed for Lomalito? How did you get my bag?"

"Shut up."

Shut up? Anger and fear fought for control of Whitehill.
He watched the jungle drift by. The not knowing was impossible to bear.

"Listen, Dr. Darreiro, I want to know what the story is here. If you're taking me back to Lomalito, great. Thank you very much. But I can't see how that's possible since you're sitting on my damn backpack that used to be in Lomalito."

"All right. All right. I'm sorry. I'm very sorry. There's nothing at all to worry about..."

"OK. Well, are we somehow heading for Lomalito?"

"Well, yes and no. Uh, we're taking a little detour, but we will wind up in Lomalito."

"Wait a second. Why the hell did you drug me last night?"

"Oh that. That was nothing. I was afraid you might not come, and I need your help."

"I think you read me correctly. I'm beat. I don't know what you've got in mind, but I don't want to go anywhere but back to Lomalito."

"I'm offering you a very rare and wonderful opportunity."

"What are you talking about? If it was so goddamn wonderful, why did you have to drug me? No. Turn around. I have to go back."

"That's not possible."

"What do you mean, 'not possible'? This is kidnapping!"

"Call a policeman."

"You're crazy."

"I'm not crazy."

"I'm going back."

"Consider the impossibility of that. You have no weapons, no food, you don't know where you are, and you can't have my canoe. Moreover, if you foolishly try to leave, I'll have Bakiratare put an arrow in some place very painful to you."

Whitehill looked back at Bakiratare, who giggled in response. "What are you doing to me here?" Dr. Darreiro caught his stroke and twisted completely around to face Whitehill. Putting his paddle across his knees, he leaned forward in a posture of earnest concentration. Whitehill wondered how the sunglasses inside his backpack were holding up.

"Oh, Mr. Whitehill. I am sorry. I've been in the jungle too long." His eyes scanned the treetops. "The heat, you know."

Dr. Darreiro pulled a tube from his breast pocket, squeezed a barrel of cream onto one finger, and rubbed the goo into his forehead. Almost immediately it was processed into chalky bubbles that lined up for the drop off the end of Dr. Darreiro's nose.

"It's difficult out here. Very interesting at first, after the initial shocks. But then it's only hard."

"Dr. Darreiro, you're not telling me anything."

"I'm trying. I'm trying. You see, when you're out there in the deep jungle, in there really, living with the Indians, the psychological burden is incredible. You need someone to elbow in the ribs once in a while and say, 'Look at that.'"

"So?"

"Well, I had to go back. The things to be seen around Bakiratare's village are too important to leave undiscovered. I was dreading going back, but when you came along I realized that if I didn't have to go alone, it would make all the difference. It was an impulse, but I couldn't take the chance you might not want to come."

Whitehill felt the man was clearly insane, or lying.

"Look, uh, Dr. Darreiro, I sympathize with you, but I'm sorry. That's just not good enough. You're taking me against my will. I want to go back."

"But don't you see? That's out of the question now. We're too far along. Past the point of no return, in a manner of speaking."

Lying. "But..."

"Please, Mr. Whitehill, no problems. Survival is a delicate matter in the jungle. If you jeopardize mine, we'll have to tie you up or something which, I assure you, will be less pleasant for both of us." Dr. Darreiro smiled thinly. "Frankly, I'm a little disappointed. I'd hoped you would be more enthusiastic. We're undertaking an extraordinary expedition. I should have thought it would appeal to you."

"Where are you taking me?"

"Stop worrying. You only have to sit back for a few days, and I'll take care of everything. You'll be escorted through unexplored territory, privileged to see people who have had no contact with the outside world, living much as they did thousands of years ago. I need to parlay with them a day or two, collect my specimens, and we'll zip right back to Lomalito..."

Whitehill stopped listening. Each stroke was taking him farther from where he wanted to be. He noted that they were moving against the current, which seemed to be weakest here, close to the bank. So the way back to Lomalito was downstream, easier.

He dismissed all he heard from Dr. Darreiro. One moment, the fellow courted his friendship; the next, he threatened to tie him up or have this Bakiratare shoot him. The drugging, the backpack from his room in Lomalito, the rare opportunity—there was no sense adding it up, because none of it figured. He was shanghaied.

The jungle laced into a wall of green on both sides of the river. It seemed less hostile, removed from the immediacy of danger here in the boat. His first choice would be stealing the canoe and heading back. He was willing to risk that much, but how could he know for sure where he might wind up? Should he play along? Unappealing as it was, Bakiratare and Dr. Darreiro were his only anchor, the only security available. Still drugged and depleted, mesmerized by the skipping glare of the sun shooting through the trees and bouncing off the water, Whitehill was unable to marshal his resolve. He would wait.

❉   ❉   ❉

Toward sundown, the energy concealed in the forest intensified, spreading behind the trees. Sharp cries answered by whistles and an occasional, invisible growl. Activity in the canoe accelerated as well. Bakiratare and Dr. Darreiro spoke more frequently.

The current became increasingly strong. Many times Whitehill's abductors switched to poles. He studied them digging in, pushing off, but offered no help.

Whenever the boat slowed, clusters of small bugs congregated at Whitehill's knees and shoulders. The more audacious of them flew down his collar, between the buttons of his shirt, under his cuffs. A small black butterfly perched on the toe of one boot. It had red piping and on each wing, incredibly, the number eighty-nine worked perfectly into a white contrasting design.

A Guest in the Jungle

Night was again reclaiming the jungle. Through mist forming on the riverbanks, he could at times make out peculiar shapes breaking the surface of the water. Darkness cooled the air, and the relief cleared Whitehill's head. For the first time that day, the muscles in his brain were able to relax, and he finally attempted to take stock of his situation.

He was a prisoner, a prisoner not only without freedom but without even the luxury of a cell or a small corner where he could retreat. And with no idea what was coming next.

"Hey!"

Bakiratare had shoved a paddle into his ribs. White-hill wheeled around, tightening his features, trying to strengthen his despair into something more formidable.

"*Yesh-ashu! Yesh-ashu!*" Bakiratare threw out his free arm, indicating that Whitehill was looking in the wrong direction.

Whitehill spun back. A short way upriver, the jungle had been cleared at a point of land more elevated than the rest. Two men waited for them just above the mud line.

Dr. Darreiro tossed his paddle into the boat and let Bakiratare guide them in. They slid neatly between several other moored canoes. The men had not moved.

Whitehill noticed that the two were not offering much of a welcome. Both had paint on their faces, something long and thin shoved through their noses, something the size of a cigarette hanging horizontally from each ear. They wore knee-length, tunic-like shirts and dark, baggy leg coverings.

Dr. Darreiro grabbed a flat brown paper package and stumbled awkwardly onto the soggy beach. His enthusiastic greeting was received impassively by the men on shore. Dr. Darreiro ripped off the end of his bundle and drew out a long machete, which he handed to the older, shorter of the two men. The other took the brown paper from Dr. Darreiro. They examined the machete without emotion, nodded in response to Dr. Darreiro's halting but long-winded monologue, and climbed back up the riverbank.

Dr. Darreiro returned to the canoe. He spoke briefly to Bakiratare and then hoisted a large green duffel bag over one shoulder.

"Cofoya Indians, Whitehill. You should find them interesting. Other than myself you'll be the only white man who's ever slept here. We'll be just the one night, so you can leave your things in the canoe if you like. No need to worry about them. There are no thieves in the interior. And in any case, Bakiratare won't be far. Fill that big pot with water and follow me."

Whitehill was relieved to stand. The hours in the canoe had bunched the cartilage in his neck, his back, and just above the knees. He stepped out of the boat, slowly stretched and twisted some of the pain. Bending to touch his toes, he noticed the muck that had gathered on his jeans. He followed the patterns of its creases up one leg as he straightened.

"Hey! The water, all right? Let's go!" Dr. Darreiro called.

"Yeah."

He reached for the pot and cautiously waded a few feet into the river. Their canoe had stirred up the area; the water was brown. One spot was as dirty as another.

"Fuck it." He dipped in, let the pot fill, and made for the top of the bank where Dr. Darreiro had disappeared.

* * *

The Cofoya village was quiet. A collection of raised wooden huts circled a central compound. Each had a frail ladder of seven or eight steps hanging off one side. Smoke seeped through the roofs and out the doors of most.

Whitehill was spotted by a group of children who ran up quickly, only to hesitate a few feet away. The taller ones boldly touched his arms and legs. They drew in more closely, grabbing for the baggier spots of his clothing, and accompanied him across the yard.

"Whitehill! In here! What are you doing?" Dr. Darreiro was bending out the doorway of a hut Whitehill had already passed. The children squealed and danced, twirling Whitehill back and guiding him to the ladder.

"All right, you guys." Whitehill smiled. "Having a little sport with old Whitehill here? Hang on one second."

He handed up the pot to Dr. Darreiro.

"Wun zecun. Wun zecun," whispered the children.

Whitehill pulled his pocket change out and distributed some coins. He shook hands with each child, saluted, and then carefully climbed the ladder. But for Dr. Darreiro's, all faces turned his way. A dozen Indians of assorted sizes rocked in hammocks; an old woman with a mound of beaded strands ringing her throat squatted next to Dr. Darreiro, poking a fire of glowing red coals.

Whitehill looked around shyly. "Hello, folks."

In a darkened corner two men echoed, "Ellu fokz, ellu fokz."

"Will you get over here, Whitehill? What is the matter with you?" Of all those in the room, Dr. Darreiro was the last person with whom Whitehill desired to share a common language. He was fascinated by the Cofoya.

"Look. Will you leave me alone? There's nothing the matter with me. You're the one with the problems."

Dr. Darreiro glanced back at the fire, then held his attention on Whitehill for a long while. "Boil that water for twenty minutes," he said softly, and left.

"Twanny minuz," repeated the two men.

Whitehill crossed to the door, curious where Dr. Darreiro was headed. Making a quick check of the village in the light that remained, Whitehill noted that the ladders of all huts were pulled in. He thought of the animals from the jungle night that might use them if they were available. Dr. Darreiro was on his way back to the canoe.

"What the fuck is with this guy?"

"Withiz-kye."

Whitehill regarded his chorus. "That's right."

"Az-rite."

"He's kidnapping me."

"Gidnappa me."

"Right."

"Rite."

In a short time others joined in, and when Dr. Darreiro returned, his arrival was attended with laughter. He silenced the room with a loud, "What's going on here?"

Whitehill looked up from his cross-legged seat by the fire. "Oh, shut up."

Quiet, until from the corner his original two-man echo tried a tentative, "Shaddup."

Dr. Darreiro walked through muffled snickers and stood over Whitehill. "Have you boiled that for twenty minutes?"

"I don't know," said Whitehill. "How long have you been gone? If you've been gone twenty minutes, it's been boiling twenty minutes."

Dr. Darreiro muttered something about hard-shelled amoebas as he picked up the pot with two sticks and set it down to cool.

Whitehill found the wood fire and the close, new smells of the hut intoxicating. The mucid air, trapped inside when a door of thick woven leaves was slid into place, began to swell with sensation. To the part of Whitehill's brain in charge of his nose, it seemed that he was in either a hayloft or a locker room on another planet.

The hut's interior was lit solely by the cooking fire. The illumination, however, was sufficient for Whitehill to make out pots and baskets, bows and arrows, machetes, and, leaning against one wall, a pair of long things that could only be blowguns. Some of the Indians still peered curiously at him from their hammocks. Most sank down deeply, stretching the weaving with their feet and shoulders, humming softly to themselves as they stared at the roof. Dr. Darreiro handed Whitehill a can of tuna fish, the lid folded back enough to scoop out meat with a finger.

"Here. Try not to make a big production out of eating, or they'll all come over and want some."

Whitehill inspected his hands and rubbed them over his shirt, rearranging the grit between his fingers. "You know, Dr. Darreiro, I still don't want to go with you. I can just stay here until you come back."

"No, you have to come."

"These people seem nice enough. I'd rather stay. See, I'm still not crazy about the way you got me here. I'm not very crazy about you, and I'm especially not crazy about going any deeper into the jungle. This is OK here. I can handle this for a couple of days. But that's it."

"No. Don't you see the favor I'm doing you? Why, already you said yourself you like these people. This is a rare and..."

"I know. I know. A wonderful opportunity. But it's no good, Dr. Darreiro. It won't wash. If I could have gotten off anywhere earlier today, I would have."

"But you can't just stay here and wait for the next bus back. What if I don't pick you up when I come back? Besides, I think I'm returning another way."

"OK. Just leave me my backpack. I think I can probably get one of these guys to give me a lift back."

Whitehill observed that Dr. Darreiro had sliced open two fingers on the jagged edges of his dinner can. Blood ran over the chunks of fish he raised to his mouth.

"Listen to me, Whitehill. I wasn't going to tell you this, but I suppose you would have discovered it anyway."

"Well? What?"

"It's emeralds. I'm not going in there to take out plant specimens. I know where there's a fortune in emeralds, and part of it is yours if you come with me."

"Emeralds? There are no stinking emeralds. And even if there were, I don't care. I still don't want to come. You're a regular loon."

"You don't believe me about the emeralds?"

"No."

"How about the plants and insects? Did you believe me about those?"

"No."

"Not even a little?"

"No! You're incredible! What the hell is going on here?"

"Look, Whitehill. I'm sorry. Maybe I made a mistake. I'm very tired. I'm going to sleep. If you still want to return in the morning, I'll take you back. All right? Happy now?"

"No. I want a better explanation."

"I said I would take you back. Now leave me alone. I'll explain tomorrow. I'm too tired now."

"Wait a second. I'd like…"

Dr. Darreiro jumped up. "I don't care what you'd like!" he screamed. "I would like to sleep!" He untangled two hammocks from the duffel bag and threw one at Whitehill.

FOUR

Ryder got out of bed and crossed to the sink. His afternoon siesta had lasted until twilight. Leaves smothering the window bounced gently on their branches, passing the last flashes of sun back and forth.

He rinsed a shot glass in the trickle from the kitchen faucet and filled it two-thirds full with Irish whiskey The maid had left a folded stack of clean towels on the table. He took one with a fading montage of Florida tourist attractions into the bathroom for his third shower of the day.

There was never a need to touch anything except the cold-water knob, but he let the spray run out of habit while tossing down his drink.

A black T-shirt was sandwiched between the towels. He recognized it as one he had sent out to be washed months ago. Two speeding hydroplanes raced over the words "New England Championships." Ryder decided on a fresh pair of jeans, pulled on his boots, brushed his teeth, grabbed his wallet. Not that there was any hurry. As a semiretired journalist, freelance explorer, and self-styled part-time adventurer, he had for several months been enjoying the consequential returns of these various professions. In short, he had no plans and no offers, which was fine.

He strolled leisurely behind the collection of shacks spread along the river's edge. A warm haze from oil lamps and charcoal stoves hung low between the sagging rooftops. When Ryder reached the old pier, he cut up to the stretch of dirt known as Boulevard de Pasteur, turning again at the Cafe Hotel.

Antonio, one of the youngest members of a small swarm of local beggars, was sneaking half-eaten biscuits off Señor John's favorite outdoor table, the one with the umbrella.

Antonio mistimed his final bold grab, and the ever watchful Señor John backhanded the boy into a carton of empty Coca-Cola bottles. Head spinning, Antonio wished now only to be allowed to run home, but Señor John had him cornered and was brandishing an old squash racket.

"Ah, Señor John," said Ryder. "Two for dinner, please."

Señor John whirled in place, unwilling to relinquish his strategic position.

"Antonio," continued Ryder, "sorry I'm late. How about a *hamburguesa*. Would that do you?"

"This boy, he's steal. He's not eat here."

"What do you mean? Antonio is my guest. Two *hamburguesas*. OK? And a beer and an orange *gaseosa*."

Señor John totaled. He lowered the squash racket. "*Papas fritas?*"

"All right."

"Two?"

"One."

"Two *hamburguesas*, one beer, one orange, one *papas fritas*."

"And ketchup this time."

"Ketchup very hard to get now. Ketchup cost you…"

"Customers never pay for ketchup on hamburgers, Senõr John."

"No? OK Two *hamburguesas*, two ketchup, one beer, one orange, two *papas fritas*."

"One *papas fritas*."

"One."

Antonio took his seat under the umbrella, beaming at this unexpected windfall. Ryder propped his boots on the short brick wall meant to inform the world where Señor John's property began. He pushed onto the back two legs of his chair, sipping contentedly from the cool beer against the humid night.

Ryder was the sort who controlled his personality by carefully choosing environments, usually those that were extreme but predictable. Life in Lomalito was easy to understand, yet everything had value or was worthy of scrutiny simply by virtue of being there. He supposed he could create a similar life in New York or London or Los Angeles, but only by learning to ignore a great deal. And when he grew bored in Lomalito, he had only to dash off a letter to Park Avenue or Earls Court or Santa Monica and imagine the recipients musing over his Amazonas postmark.

Antonio watched Ryder smiling. He smiled back and drank politely, cautious not to make any improper move that might spoil his good fortune. He scanned the street proudly, hoping one of his pals would happen by.

Señor John delivered the *hamburguesas*, ketchup already applied, and a sodden mound of french-fried potatoes greasing their paper plate to transparency.

"Hey, Senōr John. Is that guy Whitehill around?" Ryder opened his sandwich to push the tiny disk of meat onto one edge of his bun.

"*Qué?*"

"Whitehill, an American. Got here a day or two ago."

"No here."

"Here. He said he was staying at the Cafe Hotel."

"Here?" Señor John looked into the potatoes for inspiration. "Ah yes. No more. He go home."

"Home?"

"Yes, he go home. I think he get sick."

"What was wrong with him?"

"I'm not doctor. This place no easy for Americans. Miami better."

"Huh, well, too bad. When did he take off?"

"I'm going Miami next year."

"No, Whitehill."

"Oh, I think yesterday. Yes, yesterday I take him to airport. Nice man. Leave me good shirt for presents." Señor John looked back into the kitchen. "More beer?"

"Sure. Antonio, *una naranja mas?*"

Antonio nodded and bounced his feet under the table. Señor John hustled off. It was Mrs. John who reappeared with the drinks and the check.

From the mysterious inner recesses of the manager's office, the volume of the ancient Cafe Hotel sound system was cranked up on a battered and bruised Jimi Hendrix album. Señor John peeked through the crack in the door, misreading Ryder's laugh with irresolute satisfaction.

About this time, a suspiciously well-groomed Boas appeared under the street lamp, hustling toward Siete Chicas.

"Ah, Ryder! Just coming after you. Actually I wasn't, but now that I've found you, it only seems proper to take you in tow."

"What are you talking about?"

"Our mutual friend Señor McJeffers has somehow corralled a very attractive young woman at Bernardo's. She drinks *chuchuasco* respectably well... Evening, Antonio. Business must be good."

"Great, I will come along. Very considerate of you, Señor Boas." Ryder rose, counted out his dinner bill.

"Yes, actually, I should have been looking for you," said Boas. "She's interested in that peculiar professor fellow you met."

"Darreiro? The guy from the edge of town?"

"The very one. Come on then, I suppose she's too young for me anyway."

Ryder shook hands formally with Antonio and stepped back into the night.

"Say," said Boas, "let's have Señor John raise that Whitehill fellow, shall we? He should be about ready for another dose of our company."

"He left yesterday. Señor John managed to gouge him on one of his deluxe rides to the airport."

"That's unlikely."

"What do you mean?"

"I've been at the airport with McJeffers all week. European pet stores are clamoring for tropical fish, and the

Americans want snakes. We've had a number of orders to ship."

"So?"

"Well, I certainly didn't see him."

"You could have missed him."

Boas had been concentrating on a pair of candles flickering against the window of Siete Chicas, but at this he turned to look at Ryder. "How? There are only two planes a day, you know."

FIVE

Whitehill had difficulty with his hammock. He had managed to string it up his first try, deciding on a spot near the security of the fire, but could not fall asleep until he thought to imitate the Indians' diagonal position. The feeling in his arms disappeared hourly, but during scattered stretches in between, he slept.

The Cofoya rose before the sun. Even though his curiosity about them was strong, Whitehill would have chosen to remain asleep if possible. Noise, the constant jostling of his hammock, and finally thoughts about breakfast forced his eyes open. A chilly morning darkness filled the air. The same old woman coaxed flames from the smoldering coals, fanning smoke and ash about the room. Whitehill sneezed. A friendly face from the night before emerged out of the gloom and put a hand on Whitehill's hammock. "Choo," he said.

Whitehill smiled. He swung his feet over the sides of his hammock and sat up to a straddling position. The fellow handed him a banana leaf folded over what seemed to be a large white carrot. It had been cooked somehow, and the thing was warm and soft.

"*Sarra-shula.*"

Whitehill repeated, "*Sarra-shula.*" He bit in. It was terrible. Stringy and mushy at the same time. Like a potato gone mad in the jungle soil.

Dr. Darreiro's hammock was missing. Whitehill could not decide whether this was good or bad. He longed for a cup of coffee.

"*Sarra-shula.*"

"Right, *sarra-shula*," returned Whitehill, raising his breakfast in response and chewing off another inch. "*Sarra-shula.*" He twisted out of his hammock and moved sleepily to the door. A flashlight beam hit him in the face.

"Ah, just coming for you, Whitehill. I see you've discovered yucca."

"What is this stuff?"

"Yucca? It's a tuber. Grows in the ground. These cluster at the base of the plant. Has almost no nutritional value, but it fills you up."

"Wonderful."

"Do you have your hammock down yet?"

"No."

"Well, get it. Then take this torch and go down to the boat." He handed Whitehill the flashlight. "I'll meet you there."

"We're going back to Lomalito?"

"Unless you've changed your mind."

"No."

"All right. Let's get going then."

Whitehill released his slipknots. Balling the hammock under one arm, he made the rounds of the room, shaking hands with his hosts.

"So long, guys."

He jumped off the ladder and walked heavily toward the canoe. It was just light enough to do without the flashlight, but he used it anyway, playing the beam on the path before him, looking for snakes masquerading as predawn shadows. He paused at the top of the bank, looking back at the village. A small Cofoya hunting party slipped into the forest downriver.

"Come on, Whitehill. Chop chop." Dr. Darreiro was already in the bow; Bakiratare, on the beach.

Whitehill stopped in front of the boat. "Lomalito, huh?"

"Yes, that's what I said."

"You changed your mind quite easily."

"What else can I do?"

"I'm going to stay here."

"Why would you want to do that?"

"Because I don't believe you. It's impossible to believe you."

What happened next, happened fast. Dr. Darreiro barked a word to Bakiratare. Something flashed behind Whitehill, and a sting sliced above his right ear. He was on his knees, holding the blood back with both hands. Bakiratare waited, machete poised.

"I could just as easily have him kill you, Whitehill. I assure you, Bakiratare has killed many men, and one more would make little difference. He's already asked me if he could have your clothing."

Whitehill got up sluggishly, studying the blood dripping from his fingers.

"Actually, if you're going to be difficult, I would rather kill you than have to worry about you all the time. Are things clear to you now...? Fine. Get in the boat."

"Give me something to tie this off."

"The bleeding will stop. I doubt whether you're hurt that badly. Oh, all right. Get in the boat, and I'll give you some gauze. It'll be clean, at least. Apply a little pressure. That should do it."

Bakiratare circled the beach. Whitehill saw his own blood on the machete. No Cofoya had witnessed the incident. Would they have helped? He considered running back to the village. He just might be able to beat Bakiratare.

Dr. Darreiro read his thoughts. He withdrew a sawed-off shotgun from the green bag. "The boat, Whitehill. Quickly, please."

☆ ☆ ☆

They cut through a wispy fog hanging over the water. Shrill cries shouted the jungle awake. Dr. Darreiro paddled with renewed energy, working hard against the early morning coolness. Those times when Whitehill looked back at Bakiratare, he was greeted with a grin.

Sunrise was screened by the dense foliage looming over them on all sides. The canoe turned into a channel where the woods were thicker, darker, the water narrower. Lianas hung from treetops, striping the way ahead in gnarled, vertical strokes.

Plants strained over the banks, clotting into the murky river. The water made its own sound here, rushing over sticks, sliding between the leaves.

Dr. Darreiro pushed away logs and floating clumps of mud and branches blocking their way. Bakiratare stroked unbroken in a long, powerful rhythm. They traveled unspeaking through the morning. Once Dr. Darreiro passed Whitehill a canteen, once a banana. The pasty heat returned, reaching down into their green tunnel.

"*A-shiara*," said Bakiratare, "*karikatea.*" The boat was turned again, onto a shadowy stream almost hidden from view. It was necessary to lift the overhanging branches to pass. A lump of swarming black bugs fell into the canoe. Bakiratare slipped his paddle underneath and flicked them over the side. He grabbed a pole. It was possible now to push off either shore.

In a few minutes, they came to a place where the veil of woods had been cut back. Dr. Darreiro nosed the boat ashore, splashed out, and pulled them on. He unzipped his pants, urinating on the closest tree.

"Ah, the outdoors life, Whitehill. I never had much of it as a child, you know. It does something to one."

"It's certainly done something to you."

"Oh, still upset about this morning. Well, it couldn't be helped. Let's try and forget about all that. Don't do anything foolish like try for my shotgun. It's not loaded, and Bakiratare would probably whack off your arm before you even found that out."

"What's next?"

"Next? Why, next we throw some water on our faces, secure the canoe, and start walking."

"You mean there's more?"

"This is a big jungle, Whitehill. The biggest there is, as a matter of fact. From the Andes to the Atlantic. The biggest river, too. Gets as wide as eight miles. It's not the longest—the Nile has it by about four hundred Ks—but it carries the most water. The drainage basin is over two and a half million square miles. Average depth, one hundred fifty feet. Tidal bore, twelve feet..."

"All right! I mean, where are we going?"

"Why, we're going where I've been telling you we're going. Bakiratare's village."

Bakiratare had been following the conversation and smiled at the sound of his name. Whitehill turned to look at him. "Now, why would I want to go to a village full of guys who will attack me with machetes?"

"But I want you to go. Let's get ready. Long way to travel yet."

"Hmh."

"And forget about taking that pack of yours. Not only would it weigh you down, it couldn't fit. You won't need anything anyway."

"What do you mean I 'won't need anything'?"

"The people have no possessions in here. Well, nothing more than they can easily transport—weapons, pots, hammocks. Nothing like what you have in there."

"How do you know what I have?"

"I looked."

Whitehill unzipped the bag. From the crushed and flattened contents, he pulled out a long-sleeved denim shirt, sweat socks, vitamin pills, toothbrush, Band-Aids, and a pair of khaki Brooks Brothers pants. He removed his sleeping bag from its stuff sack, fastened the bag to the pack frame, and replaced it with his selections.

"Come on!"

Ignoring Dr. Darreiro, Whitehill carefully secured the sack to his belt and retied his boots. He zipped his soggy passport and traveler's checks in a side compartment of the backpack.

"Let's go! Here. You'll need these." Dr. Darreiro tossed Whitehill a knit hat and a pair of work gloves.

"What for?"

"The gloves because you'll fall constantly, and the cap because your hair will catch in the branches."

Bakiratare hacked at the plants and trees around the canoe, neatly camouflaging the spot in minutes. Dr. Darreiro had a canvas bag strapped tightly to his shoulders. He unslung it.

"As long as you have room, take these," said Dr. Darreiro, handing Whitehill a few cans of sardines and a brown package the size of a quart of milk.

"I don't have much room. What is that?"

"Nothing exotic. Colored thread. They use it for their arrows. Oh, and you better start your Aralen." He opened a small jar and shook a pile of pink pills into Whitehill's hand. "For malaria, one a week."

Bakiratare rushed forward eagerly. Dr. Darreiro handed him a white pill from another jar. "Aspirin," he said to Whitehill. "Malaria medicine won't do him any good. The Indians could never get enough. They do love to take pills, however. Let's be off."

The largest butterfly Whitehill had ever seen fluttered down into the clearing. Ice blue with a leisurely, rolling motion that made the insect look like a sheet of paper caught in a breeze. When the sun turned it against the leaves, the effect was extraordinary.

"Extraordinary, eh?" said Dr. Darreiro. He walked to the edge of the forest. Bakiratare passed him, slashing into the brush with short, whistling chops. The suggestion of a path appeared behind him. Dr. Darreiro swept his hand to the opening. "You're next, Whitehill."

*　*　*

Whitehill stepped into the jungle. He felt swallowed.

It was as Dr. Darreiro had described. Every few steps, Whitehill tripped. He was at first reluctant to grab out blindly in an effort to stop his fall. Soon he became less cautious, reaching for branches, bracing himself against tree trunks.

The overhanging boughs dipped to a few feet from the ground. Sometimes the trio climbed over, sometimes squatted under. Going around was out of the question since the limbs vanished into the jungle on both sides of the trail.

Their route took them up and down hills. As the angles steepened, Dr. Darreiro and Whitehill switched to climbing, gaining hold on a root or stout plant and using the footprints of the man ahead as steps. Bakiratare merely bent deeper, thwacking down the growth, pushing it aside.

Downhill was more difficult. The underbrush clawed Whitehill below the chin, poked his rib cage. The loose footing turned each step into a slide. He caught at vines to steady himself.

At the base of the hills, there was usually water. Mostly it was a clear trickle that could be sucked on hands and knees. When it was a river, the crossing was difficult, but then it was possible to see the sky. The currents became stronger.

Once they had to cross a rough, muddy bog by tight-roping over a fallen tree. Into the rhythm of their march,

Whitehill barely hesitated. He knew, however, that if there were such a thing as quicksand, this must be it. Whitehill's thighs began quivering. He thought now mainly about resting but would not allow himself to be the first to suggest it. Behind him, Dr. Darreiro twanged strange, high-pitched animal grunts but was uncomplaining. Energized by that strength so characteristic of madmen, he kept coming.

They topped one of the large hills and joined a wider trail. The terrain was equally formidable, but hiking became easier. Others had beaten back the jungle. The path seemed to be maintained.

Bakiratare grabbed Whitehill by the arm. "What is it?" panted Dr. Darreiro. Bakiratare raised his hand for silence. He pointed several feet ahead where an anteater had frozen in profile. To Whitehill, it looked exactly the way an anteater was supposed to look. Bakiratare threw a rock at it, laughed, and looked to his companions for approval. Whitehill, happy for a chance to relax, smiled and nodded. Dr. Darreiro snorted. "Come on! *Yaka!*"

Leaf-cutter ants were in abundance, parading single file over anything in their way, carrying their harvest overhead. They looked like a salad moving through the jungle, the guards riding atop the sliced leaves, testing the air with their antennae. It was a good place to be an anteater.

Later that day, they stopped once more. Bakiratare held up his hands and walked off the trail. Whitehill heard the sounds of a machete, and Bakiratare returned with a pole twice as long as he was.

"What's happening?" asked Whitehill.

"Stand still. Snake."

A thick brown snake lay quietly coiled in their path. "Must be asleep," said Dr. Darreiro.

Bakiratare silently moved in closer, brought the staff back over his shoulders, and whipped it down on the snake's head. He jumped away as the reptile exploded in spasmodic, writhing loops. When the power was drained from its frantic thrusts, Bakiratare sliced through behind the jaws. He pushed the pole between coils and, laughing, lifted it over his head. Both ends still touched the ground.

"Snakes have notoriously thin skulls," said Dr. Darreiro. "It's the rule of the road in here to kill snakes, because the next party passing through might not see them."

Whitehill was too exhausted to be frightened by the incident. He was glad for the break. Dr. Darreiro sat back against a tree. Whitehill went straight down, settling in the middle of the trail.

"I think we've earned five minutes' rest," said Dr. Darreiro. "That, by the way, was a bushmaster, a fairly large one. *Lachesis muta*, I believe. Of the pit viper family."

"Attractive name."

"Isn't it? Has nothing to do with a pit in the ground. It's those little things behind the nostrils. They're heat-sensing membranes stretched over tiny pits. Useful in hunting. If this one had bitten you, the venom would have broken down the blood vessels, stopped your blood from clotting. Immediate pain and swelling." Dr. Darreiro smiled intently at Whitehill. "They can strike about two-thirds of their body length. He would have hit you somewhere around your neck, I would think. Probably knock you off this little mountain. You would have fallen through the jungle, flailing away at this snake whose fangs were sunk deep in your throat.

The two of you, tangled in each other, rolling to the bottom while you began to bleed through most of the pores in your body—your nose, under the fingernails, your eyes."

"Sorry to deprive you of a show."

"Oh, you haven't necessarily. That head can still deliver venom for another half hour at least."

"Very tempting. Care to roll up your sleeve?"

"Whitehill! Bakiratare and I just saved your life."

"You fellows are too good to me."

"I would have thought some gratitude might be appropriate. You can see how hopeless you would be in here on your own."

"I wouldn't be in here if it weren't for you! Like to tell me what's going on now? Why I'm getting this exclusive guided tour?"

"But I have told you. Emeralds. These hills are full of emeralds."

"Will you stop with the emeralds already? You don't kidnap someone so you can force a fortune in emeralds down his throat."

"All right! So there are no emeralds. It's plants and insects."

"You're a maniac! I'm trapped in the middle of the Amazon at the mercy of a maniac!"

"That does seem to be the case."

"Yes it does."

"How about if I had only said plants? Would you have believed that?"

"Aaaaah!"

"No, I suppose not. Don't call me a maniac, please. I find it most insulting."

"You do? I apologize. I certainly have no reason to upset you."

"Fine. Let's push on now, shall we?"

Bakiratare tossed the snake into the woods and led the way. Although the sun would not set for an hour or more, the jungle was already becoming dark. Bakiratare had cut his pole to manageable size, using it to probe the trail ahead.

"Just around the bend, Whitehill. We can stop now."

They had come to an area where the jungle seemed to have been bombed. Blackened trees lay on their sides, splayed about broken and charred stumps.

"What…?"

"Used to be a garden. They burn it to clear it."

At one end, thin poles held up a roof of leaves. Dr. Darreiro distributed hammocks, and the three spaced them underneath.

"You're in the middle, Whitehill."

"I figured."

Dinner for each was a can of sardines washed down and washed off with water at a nearby stream. Walking back to their shelter, Bakiratare plucked a bunch of bananas and passed them around.

Dr. Darreiro pulled out a length of plastic twine. "I'm most sorry to have to do this, Whitehill, but I won't sleep well unless I do."

"Do what?"

"I'm afraid I'm going to have to tie you up."

"Tie me up!"

"Not all of you, of course. Only your hands."

"You're tying me up?"

"If I don't tie you up, you may decide to wander off, and you'd probably injure yourself."

"Look, I'm too beat to stand. I'm not going to run around the jungle at night."

"No, I doubt if you would. But you might."

"You're not tying me up, you fucking lunatic."

"If you don't allow me to do this easily, I'll tell Bakiratare to hit you with his machete. It will hurt. I'll continue to have him do so until you climb gratefully into your hammock."

Bakiratare advanced. Whitehill measured him. He could fend off one swipe of the machete with his arm. Then he would kick the little shit between the legs as hard as possible. If not that, an uppercut with his uninjured arm, a punch that was likely to land somewhere.

"The ideal weapon for the jungle, Whitehill." Dr. Darreiro aimed at his stomach. 'You saw off the barrel so it doesn't get hung up in the branches. Makes it easy to carry. And the scatter pattern of the shot makes it difficult to miss."

Bakiratare took advantage of Whitehill's switch in attention to lash into his side. The blade bit to the bone in his hip.

"Ow! Dammit! Fuck!"

"That will be no problem to wrap. I have more gauze, and you can tie it around your waist."

"All right! All right! Jesus Christ! You're fucking insane!" Whitehill reasoned that it would be pointless to make a stand at this time. It was dark, he was exhausted, and there was no element of surprise. He bandaged his wound and collapsed into the middle hammock.

"I asked you not to call me names, Whitehill. I won't warn you again. Put your hands in back of you."

Dr. Darreiro worked the rope into the weave of White-hill's hammock. His hands were bound together and secured behind as well. If an emergency should arise, he would be helpless. At least his position in the middle hammock afforded him some degree of protection.

"Now, Whitehill, a final humanitarian gesture." Dr. Darreiro unbuttoned his shirt pocket, removed a spray can, and shot into Whitehill's face. "Insect repellent. Don't worry."

Thus protected from the dangers of the Amazon by a filmy layer of chemicals, Whitehill accepted the sanctuary of sleep.

SIX

When Whitehill awoke, his hands were raw and pitted with rope burns. Dr. Darreiro had either forgotten to protect his own face or sweated off the insect spray, because one cheek was misshapen with red bumps. Bakiratare sat between a small fire and a mound of banana skins, singing in muffled soprano.

"You'd never believe you could feel chilly in here, would you, Whitehill? Amazes me every morning. Like the desert in some ways. As a matter off fact, the Sahara…"

"I don't want to hear about the Sahara."

"You don't? Why, it actually freezes there sometimes. Temperature plummets at night. The diurnal range is usually eighty or ninety degrees. Of course, it also happens to be the hottest place in the world. A hundred thirty-six degrees in the shade one time in 1922."

"Will you please untie me?"

"Of course. Of course. Right. Can't stay in the hammock all day."

Dr. Darreiro fooled with the knots at Whitehill's wrists, eventually electing to slice them apart. "Don't like to do that. Everything is precious in here. Long rope more valuable than short. I suppose I have enough. Eat some bananas."

Whitehill rubbed his hands awake while toasting them over the fire. Shadows thinned and dissolved; familiar noises returned. He peeled and swallowed as many bananas as he could contain.

"It's light enough to start. Let's get going. Come on, Whitehill. Take your hammock down. I won't be responsible for your hammock."

"I want to change my clothes."

"Why? That's ridiculous. Anything you put on will just get dirty again."

"These are disintegrating on me. They're so ripped, the ends that hang out keep getting caught. It slows me down, it's aggravating, and changing clothes is not that big a deal."

"Fine. Fine. We'll wash in the stream. You can change there."

Whitehill drank at the stream. He rinsed his hands and held them against his face. "I'd like to change my bandage."

"Out of the question. No time. No bandage."

Untying his stuff sack, Whitehill pulled out the fresh change of clothes. He laid them flat and began to unbutton his shirt. Bakiratare stared at Whitehill. Dr. Darreiro stared at the clothes.

"Are those Brooks Brothers pants?"

"Yes, they happen to be Brooks Brothers pants. They're very lightweight, and they dry a lot quicker than jeans." Whitehill started undoing his belt. "Hey, can I have a little privacy here?"

"Oh, my dear Whitehill."

"Look at the way he's staring at me. I feel like Jayne Mansfield at a truck stop."

"Ha. I suppose you're entitled. Take your privacy."

Whitehill trudged up to the shelter. He changed his pants and socks, retied his shoes, and he was off. Softly at first, skimming across the clearing, then racing back down the trail. Whispering to himself, "Come on, Whitehill! Come on! Go, boy! Go go go!"

He flew—jumping, hurdling, ducking. There was no question of caution now, and boldness smoothed his flight through the jungle. It was not just that Whitehill was afraid, but for the first time in what seemed like a very long time, he was acting for himself, choosing the speed and direction of his own body across the surface of the planet. The leaves slipped by, flicking off his cheeks and shoulders. For this moment, at least, he was free. The result was exhilarating, and he didn't want to lose it. He welcomed the pain and fatigue as a challenge. "C'monnnnn, Whitehill."

Arms and legs pumping, he felt in a state of constant acceleration. He heard nothing behind. "All right! I'm cleanin' those guys, man. Wooo!" Strains of the "William Tell Overture" seeped through his cerebrum. Whitehill was motoring. A branch path appeared to his right, and he turned. It was tighter, but Whitehill bounced through, a boxer, dodging and weaving, blocking off branches in his way.

Suddenly there was a river. He splashed in. The current was strong, but the water refreshed him, and, running and stroking, he plowed to the other side. Another kind of path here. Clean lines, sharper and true. Whitehill hazarded a look behind. "Oh no!" Bakiratare was entering the river, a red-faced Dr. Darreiro in his wake, coming up fast.

"That's impossible. I don't believe it. I should be way ahead." He was off again. A little less confident, but still quick. This path followed a different direction, running parallel to the riverbank. A fork, one way slanting deeper into the jungle. Whitehill took it while reexamining his tactics. Bakiratare could probably keep this up all day, and there was no telling what reserves were bottled up inside Dr. Darreiro. All right, then. The path had some sharp turns. When Whitehill was certain he was out of sight of his pursuers, he dived in. The leaves closed over him. Whitehill's hands touched soft ground. He turned a half somersault and froze.

A few seconds later Bakiratare ran by, then Dr. Darreiro, grunting, "Ye, ye, ye, ye, ye."

Whitehill was silent. Various members of the resident insect population discovered his hiding place, but he fought off only the most annoying, and even these were dispatched noiselessly. He listened to his own breath escaping and entering, monitored his heartbeat.

They came back, Bakiratare ahead. There was a sharp edge to their conversation. Whitehill understood nothing but was sure he knew what was being discussed. Through the leaves he had a glimpse of Dr. Darreiro's shoe, a slice of stocking, the bottom of a muddy pants leg. They retraced their steps toward the river and returned, passing within a yard of Whitehill's nose. The two made another pass. Somehow, they were convinced he was in this general area.

Whitehill could see them almost clearly at times. They were not far down the trail. Bakiratare stared about nervously. Dr. Darreiro pushed around the brush, peering off the path. Both were slowly heading his way. Whitehill remained absolutely still. He had a hand over his nose and mouth. His eyes followed them in. They were very close now. The arrow that killed Bakiratare caught him straight on, right in the solar plexus. A barbed arrowhead popped out his back. He held the shaft, sat down, and fell over. Dr. Darreiro's jaws stretched open in terror, the scream trapped in his throat. A bug flew in. "Ach! Ptoo, ptoo, gaa!" He fled to the river.

Whitehill stayed beneath the leaves. He followed Dr. Darreiro's noises until they were lost in the rustles, buzzes, and shrieks of the jungle. Bakiratare's body pulsed around the arrow in his chest. An Indian emerged from the trees. He resembled Bakiratare but was nearer Whitehill's own size. One arm wrapped around a bow and a sheaf of arrows, one hand scratched a mop of dark hair. He stared directly at the spot where Whitehill lay. When he turned to look at Bakiratare, Whitehill balanced on his hands, pulled his knees under him.

The Indian squatted, bit his lower lip. Using the arrow as a lever, he flipped Bakiratare onto his back. The arrowhead was forced backward, tiny spouts of blood percolated from the wound. He stood and scratched his head again. "Damn! OK, *hombre. Sírvase venir acá...venha cá por favor...*" He walked to the brush, where Whitehill crouched in an unsuccessful attempt to make himself smaller. "*Esta bien...está bem...hola, amigo...bom dia...alabado...*hello in there."

Whitehill came forward. The Indian allowed himself part of a smile. "*Quiere usted darme su nombre?*"

"*Yo soy...*uh, *un hombre...*um...I'm..."

"English? You're an American. What are you doing here? Who are you?"

"Me?"

"I don't mean some fellow over in China."

"I am an American, a traveler. Those two were kidnapping me, and I was trying to escape."

"Kidnapping you?"

"I don't know what else to call it."

"Why?"

"I don't know why."

The Indian nodded toward Bakiratare. "It had to have been something pretty important, or he would have never crossed that river. Who was the other one?"

"His name's Dr. Darreiro. I don't know very much about him. He's got a place outside Lomalito."

"Lomalito? And these two were together? He spoke their language?"

"Yeah."

"And they were holding you prisoner?"

"Tied me up, the whole deal. They even cut me with a machete when I wouldn't cooperate."

"But they must not have wanted to kill you because our friend here could have easily dropped you with an arrow crossing the river."

"He could?"

"Yes, he could. It looks like he managed to do a nice job behind your ear. You've got an infection working there, you know."

"Great. Wait a minute. What are you doing speaking English?"

The Indian laughed. "I was wondering when you'd get to that. Here, let me show you something." He pointed to one of Bakiratare's feet. "This is probably what saved you."

"What?"

"Look closely at his big toe."

Whitehill bent over the body. On the inside tip of Bakiratare's toe were a pair of tiny holes, perfectly round, no more than an eighth inch in diameter. "What are these?"

"Your friend was attacked by vampire bats last night. There's another bite on his elbow."

"But there's no blood."

"No. On the wound, there never is. And the one being bitten never knows until morning. I don't think I've ever heard of someone waking and catching them in the act."

Whitehill shuddered. "So how did that save me?"

"When the bats feed off you, they draw huge amounts of blood. Much more than you'd imagine by looking at them. They pull out the nutrients, and the rest passes through. Two bites tapped out at least enough to weaken him. Probably enough to make him dizzy. He'd have caught you otherwise. You don't feel any different?"

"I don't think so."

"You slept in your shoes?"

"Yes."

"Check your hands."

"My hands were tied under me."

"There you are. They can get you on the nose or forehead, too, but I don't see anything... Are those Brooks Brothers pants you have on?"

"Yes." Whitehill's thoughts were wrapped tightly around the possibility of a vampire bat hovering silently over his nose the night before. Maybe he should have just gone to an island somewhere. Lain on a beach for a few months. Or back to Europe. That had been a nice vacation. Or taken a cabin in the mountains… But what was most chilling was that they sink their little vampire teeth into you, and you don't feel it. You don't wake up. You just sleep on, your nose attached to a bat's teeth. He gazed absently at the Indian, who balanced against the long bow, wearing only a loincloth the size of an airline ticket. "How did you know these were Brooks Brothers pants? No, no, just forget that a second. I'm interested in that. I do want to know that. But what I really want to know is why you shot him."

"I had no choice. He entered our territory. Crossing that river is an act of aggression. He knew that. Which brings us back to you. Clearly, there's some powerful stuff going down that you're tied into, or he wouldn't have taken the risk."

"What? Why were they doing this to me?"

"I'm not sure, but you can be fairly certain that yours was a one-way ride."

"You mean they were going to kill me?"

"Not such an unlikely occurrence in the jungle. Anyway, you looked like you can move through the woods fast enough, so knock that spider off your leg and follow me."

"Yah! Hey, hold on!"

But the Indian was already bounding up the trail. White-hill fell in behind, puffing and muttering to himself. It was true that he had become more agile, jogging and picking his way along jungle trails. And he was continually seeing things he'd never seen before—a cloud of butterflies blocking the sun as they crossed a river, a cone-shaped burst of bright orange flowers. The bottom line, however, was that he was getting goddamn tired of running through the jungle all the time. How long had it been? The forest seemed to suspend each moment in deliberate, curious ways.

Whitehill concerned himself with short patches of time, small distances. Get past that tree; get through these brambles. Push hard for five minutes; let up for the next five.

And who the hell was this guy? "Hey! Hey, wait a minute, will you? Who are you?"

The Indian stopped and grinned at Whitehill. He pulled a small machete from the string holding his loincloth. "Aterarana. You?"

"Whitehill."

"Here, Whitehill." Aterarana cut down a stick, split it in two. Stringy white inside, but sweet and moist.

"Thanks. Umm. Listen, Aterarana, it's very nice to meet you. And thanks for saving my life. I appreciate that. But I still have about seven thousand questions I'd like to ask you. Please understand, I'm not trying to be ungrateful. It's just that for quite a while now I haven't had the slightest idea what was happening to me. And this business about the pants…"

"Don't worry, pal. I understand perfectly. But you've got to hold on a little. I just killed somebody, remember. And there seem to be things of huge importance happening around here, here also being where I live. What I'm trying to do now is head back home as quickly as possible so I can kick this around with the chief and everybody else and try and make some sense of it. I know it's tough, but you're going to have to be patient. As far as the pants go, they were always a little baggy for my taste. We don't have much farther to travel. OK? Let's hit it. You can carry the bow if you want."

"What? Why would I want to carry the bow?"

"I thought you might want to pretend you're an Indian... Only kidding, kidding. Just trying to loosen things up a bit. Hey, you've got to admit you're better off now than you were an hour ago."

"Boy, I hope so."

"You're free to go at any time."

"Now where am I going to go?"

"Another little joke."

"*Little* is the word."

"Jungle humor. All set? We're off."

Whitehill cast a glance heavenward. "This is what you send me? A comedian?"

* * *

Perched quietly overhead, the monkey watched two men pass. The Indian, swift and light, moving like the wind, and the lawyer from Pittsburgh, battered and bruised and losing the crease in his Brooks Brothers pants. High as his vantage point was, the monkey still lost sight of the men in seconds. Instinctively, he howled after them as they disappeared, slipping deeper into the forest.

SEVEN

The streets of Bogotá are divided into *calles* and *carreras* that run perpendicular to one another. An address of *calle* 5, number 10–15 means proceed to the intersection of *calle* 5 and *carrera* 10, then walk toward *carrera* 11 to find the structure marked 15.

Frustrated by the sensible organization of their city, Bogotá drivers, descendants for the most part of adventurous Spaniards, must honk their horns in continual protest. The casual visitor might guess that the black smoke they release is responsible for the haze overhead, but he would be only partially correct. Bogotá is always overcast, always chilly and wet, and always at 8,700 feet.

The serious young men of Bogotá wrap thick scarves around their necks and are fortunate enough to walk the streets with the world's most beautiful women, save perhaps those in certain pockets of the Middle East, Scandinavia, and a couple of other locations that cannot be disclosed.

At most corners, someone will raise a carton of cigarettes from the folds of his *ruana* and shout, "Marlboro! Marlboro!"

A Guest in the Jungle

A warning in the *South American Handbook* reads, "Pickpockets and thieves are notorious in Bogotá. Watch your money and valuables closely; don't wear personal jewelry, take your glasses off if you can see without them, and NEVER walk into a crowd." There are persistent rumors of schools for pickpockets on the outskirts of Bogotá and grisly tales of professionals who maim infants to make them more pitifully successful beggars. Beyond the dishonest are a group of harmless, wandering derelicts whom the same casual visitor might mistake for these thieves but who are not.

And not everyone stalking the street is interested in the contents of his neighbor's pockets. It must be argued that this sophisticated colonial city has its charm, the "Athens of Latin America." But it is a foolish driver indeed who attempts to negotiate the *carreras* and *calles* with his window down and his watch on the left hand.

* * *

Tavars tapped the currency conversion into his pocket calculator. Forty-two dollars. Too much for a ride in from the airport. He set an eight a.m. alarm on the digital clock residing in the calculator's microchips and absentmindedly replaced it inside his briefcase.

Somewhere between New York and Bogotá, the airlines had misplaced his suitcase. The Miami–Bogotá connection had been delayed, then diverted to Barranquilla, where passengers were switched to a prop plane bound for Medellín. Tavars spent his afternoon shuffling about the airport, drinking tiny cups of black coffee, washing his face in the

78

restroom, and arguing with airline officials. They told him the airport in Bogotá was broken.

When Tavars had finally arrived at the Hotel Tequendama in Bogotá, he had immediately telephoned Señor García, but the office was closed for the day. Just as well. Tavars had underestimated the effects of the altitude and welcomed an opportunity to rest.

He was not pleased with his hotel room. It was neither big enough nor elegant enough. It smelled funny. He parted the heavy drapes, exposing Bogotá, which twinkled fifteen floors below. "From up here, they all look good," Tavars said aloud. He needed a drink.

The phone smelled funny, too. "Hello. Hello. I want room service. *Servicio.* Yes? I want a glass of white wine and a ham sandwich. OK? Ham sandwich. Yes? Good-bye."

Service was prompt, but the wine was warm and the ham ice-cold. He ate anyway and was sorry for it. The wine had smelled funny.

Deciding upon fresh air as the remedy for all the forces mistreating his body, he combed his hair, smoothed his jacket, and ventured into the hallway. Elevator doors opened, and he switched places with a very fat man squeezing past. Tavars pushed the lobby button, but the car went up two floors. A name-tagged group rushed aboard, forcing him into a corner. Mercifully, the elevator began its descent.

"Earl, where are John and Helen?"

"They said they would meet us in the lobby."

"Bud, is that you back there? I thought you'd still be at dinner."

Hearty laughter. The doors opened and a beaming, middle-aged couple labeled John and Helen greeted their arrival. "What took you so long?"

"Oh, Bud had to stop on the way to get something to eat."

Laughter all around. Tavars pushed through and stomped outside. The air was too thin and textured with soot.

"Hello, sir. Hello."

"Yes?"

"I am leaving tomorrow for the salt cathedral. Small group. Very exclusive."

"Salt cathedral?"

"Yes, lunch included, returning in the afternoon."

"No, I'm sorry. Thank you."

"Yes? Very reasonable."

"No. I said no." Tavars was mildly curious as to why these people should worship salt, but he had the good sense not to try extracting any information from this fellow. He allowed a brochure to be pressed into his hand and dropped it crossing the street.

"Eight a.m., sir. Assembling here. Executive motor coach."

"No!"

Tavars listened to automobiles calling, challenging each other. There was never a time when a horn was not being pushed somewhere—a blaring, shifting backdrop constantly rearranging itself at intersections all over town. He looked back at the Tequendama, tried to pick out his room. Had he left the light on?

The delicate evening drizzle had begun to string out his hair. He felt short of breath. Nonetheless, Tavars made a pact with himself to walk all around this block.

"Marlboro?"

"No!"

Closing his eyes, Tavars pinched a thumb and forefinger into the bridge of his nose. He increased the pressure for a count of ten, slackened off to a count of five more. When Tavars looked up, he saw a hippie walking toward him—Fu Manchu mustache, tennis shoes, backpack, red hair. One of the worst kind.

Suddenly, two men appeared behind the hippie, each locking onto an arm. A third knocked past Tavars, dug into the hippie's shirt, and ripped out a leather pouch.

"Hey! Hey! Stop!"

The three men fled in different directions.

"Hey! Help! My passport! My money!"

Tavars pretended not to understand.

The hippie ran after the third man, fifty pounds of pack bouncing into the small of his back. A Canadian flag was stitched on the flap. The backpack was slung down, and the hippie accelerated into the chase. One of the first men emerged from an alley, grabbed the backpack, and ran in the opposite direction.

"Canadians," thought Tavars, "Colombians." He hastened back to his room, swallowed a Valium, slept badly, woke too soon, and watched morning slip under the curtains.

✻　✻　✻

The room had grown cold during the night. A splendid silk robe that Tavars would have worn had been sold hours before in Barranquilla as the major part of a deal that also included three custom-made shirts, two neckties, and some very thin socks. His bag was purchased by a smuggler who expertly read into its smooth leather lines and elegant clasps the possibilities of sophisticated deception. No one bought the underwear. Years later, Manuel Ríos, the baggage handler who originally appropriated the suitcase, would be found stabbed to death in a Santa Marta alleyway wearing only a pair of Saks Fifth Avenue boxer shorts.

"Hello? Hello!"

"Good morning, sir."

"Yes. Get me 24 17 00."

"Again, please."

"Two four one seven oh oh."

"…Banco de la Moneda."

"I want to speak to Señor García."

"One moment."

Tavars impatiently tucked the bedcovers tightly at his sides. The phone sizzled and popped. A smooth female voice said something he could not understand.

"Señor García, please."

"Señor García is not in."

"Well, when is he due?"

"I don't know, sir."

"This is very important. I had an appointment with Señor García yesterday and…"

"Is this Mr. Tavars?"

"Yes. Yes, it is."

"You missed your plane."

"No, my plane was ten hours late. I…"

"We know, Mr. Tavars. Señor García will be expecting you at four o'clock."

"Four o'clock? I need to see him earlier."

"I'm sorry."

"Can you reach him for me?"

"We will send a car for you at a quarter to four."

"But…oh, all right."

"Good-bye, Mr. Tavars."

"Good-bye."

Tavars showered, climbed reluctantly into yesterday's clothes, called his travel agent in New York to complain about the suitcase, and left the hotel in poor spirits. He entered the first restaurant that looked tolerably clean. Although no word of understanding passed between him and the waitress, he was presented with a delicious surprise of eggs, onion, and tomato in a small casserole. Tavars returned to the hotel, bought a book he would have been embarrassed to read at home, and spent a bearable morning in his room. He ordered a disappointing steak sandwich, slept it off, showered again, and was downstairs by three thirty.

A small orange van pulled up to the main door, depositing John, Helen, Bud, Earl, many others Tavars did not recognize, and one more that he did.

"Hello, sir. Hello. Remember me, sir?"

Tavars nodded.

"Salt cathedral."

"Yes, yes."

"You wish to go tomorrow?"

"No."

"Very reasonable."

The salt cathedral man looked at Tavars as if he were very strange indeed. This American had closed his eyes and was squeezing his nose, hard. He watched for a moment as the veins in this man's forehead presented themselves, but the salt cathedral man chose not to become involved in such strangeness. He left in pursuit of his flock. "Mr. Bud! Mr. Earl! Wait, please!"

At twenty minutes past four, a highly polished, silver-blue Mercedes with tinted windows drove around the vehicles at the entrance of the Tequendama and onto the sidewalk. A thin, sleepy man in a charcoal uniform came out of the driver's side.

"Señor Tavars," he said to no one in particular.

Tavars identified himself and was ushered into the back seat. At the Banco de la Moneda, he was met by an over-dressed guard who escorted Tavars up to the top floor and handed him over to a trim, attractive young woman.

"Good afternoon, Mr. Tavars."

"Good afternoon."

"You're late. You may go right in."

Tavars could not decide if there was intended irony in that lateness remark. Her smile seemed relaxed, and her swept-back hair revealed so much of her face and neck that she appeared…

"Mr. Tavars!"

"Señor García. Good afternoon."

"I'm sorry, Mr. Tavars, but you can't have Miss Salcedo. I have tried myself. But she's new. There is time. Come in."

Señor García latched onto a bit of Tavars's jacket, guiding him through the double doors. He watched Miss Salcedo return to the reception area, and slid a hefty bolt into place.

"Please sit down, Mr. Tavars."

The high-ceilinged office was paneled in a bright, rust-colored wood, which Tavars could not identify. Enormous windows were spaced along the two walls that formed the corner behind Señor García's desk. A black leather chair meant for visitors was too soft for Tavars, but he adjusted.

García was thicker and darker than Tavars had remembered. "You drink Cognac, Mr. Tavars?"

"Well, yes I do, but…"

Two women entered through a side door. They opened a mirror-lined cabinet, fixed two tulip-shaped glasses, and balanced these along with an ebony humidor on a golden tray.

"You smoke cigars, Mr. Tavars?"

"I do smoke cigars."

"Cuban. I don't imagine you get them very often. The Cognac is Delamain." He admired the liquid's pale sparkle against the black and gold. "Pleasantly dry."

Tavars nodded.

"These two speak no English. We may talk freely. The one with blond hair is Betty." Betty smiled, handed Tavars a drink, and lit his cigar. "Do you like her?"

"Pardon me?"

"Betty. Do you like her?"

"Why yes, she seems very nice."

García mumbled something to the other woman, who crossed to his side of the desk and disappeared underneath. Betty knelt at Tavars's feet and reached for his belt.

"What…?"

"Southern hospitality, Mr. Tavars. Your Mr. Schaffer did as much for me our last meeting in Las Vegas. It is quite usual. Do you wish to switch?"

"No, I just…"

Betty had his waistband loosened, and Tavars involuntarily rose from the chair as she pulled his pants and shorts down to the knees in one swift move. He turned meekly to his host, but García was concentrating elsewhere for the moment. Betty purred at the softness between Tavars's legs and began to coax it with her tongue. He gulped at his Cognac. His glass was so thin there was a real possibility he might snap off the rim.

"So, Mr. Tavars, I hope we can agree on finalizing this project."

"Uh-huh."

"I must say that we here are growing impatient and see little need for further delays."

"Uh-huh, um, we recently received, uh, a little while ago, a cable from Darreiro."

"Darreiro again. Darreiro is a needless precaution. A hindrance. Also, I find him strange."

Betty's hands drew Tavars out in long, firm strokes. She wet two fingers and painted him with her saliva as she admired her work. When Tavars began to speak, she laced her hands behind him and with surprising strength pulled him into her mouth.

"Darreiro, uh, just needs a little more time."

"But why bother? We can finish the job at any time."

"Señor García, we have, in America, uh, pressure groups. People concerned about things like forests and whales."

"Whales?"

"Well, anything. You know, with environment or refugees or some cause. But the point is they watch companies like ours very closely, and if they don't like what they see, they make trouble."

"But they watch you in America, and we are talking about the Amazon jungle."

"A hint of anything, anything seen, a rumor, a speck of evidence. Newspapers live for these things, and for us they translate into hundreds of millions of dollars, or jail."

"You worry about nothing."

It might have been that Betty was growing careless with her teeth, but Tavars squirmed, uncomplaining. He studied her head bobbing in rhythm. "One never knows who's roaming around, umh, in the jungle."

"This jungle, Mr. Tavars, is unexplored. Except for these Indians, it's uninhabited. And proving anything is an impossible matter altogether."

"But planes, Señor García. They take off; they land. People fly them. People see them. We feel…"

García seized a handful of his woman's hair and pulled her off just before his climax. In his mind, the matter had been decided. He would allow Tavars's people a few more days, out of courtesy, and then proceed his own way. It was tiresome working with Americans, but they did have considerable power. There was nothing more to gain by prolonging this exchange. He regarded his guest. "You take drugs, Mr. Tavars?"

* * *

A few blocks away, and many floors below, Bud was walking back from the Gold Museum. Unable to nap, he had ventured out on his own that afternoon and was thinking up adjectives that would impress the others with what they had missed. He arrived at the Tequendama just as a Mercedes steered in, and as things happen on vacation, he saw that same fellow again, the one from the elevator who had also been there when they got back after the salt cathedral and now, getting dropped off in a Mercedes! Another tidbit that the others had missed. Bud was going to wow them at dinner tonight.

* * *

Miss Salcedo arrived home at sunset. Her front door was unlocked, the fireplace alive, and a bottle of dark wine open on the desk. Ryder had made himself at home without difficulty, a talent he'd developed of necessity over the years.

Since meeting this woman in Siete Chicas, things had moved rapidly. Through a *chuchuasco*-induced haze, he had been unable to determine exactly who had seduced whom. But he'd not been regretful in the morning and, intrigued, had accompanied her back to Bogotá with few second thoughts.

She took a cassette from her purse and tossed it to him. "You got it?"

"Some," she said, kicking off her shoes. "We still don't know where, and we still don't know when, but I think you'll find it interesting listening."

"Is Tavars linked up with Darreiro?"

"Yes. He's also a slob. He looked like he hadn't changed his clothes in a week."

"Anything else?"

"Uh-huh, but it's pretty tangled...and then there's still that guy Whitehill."

"Yeah," said Ryder, "there's still Whitehill."

EIGHT

There's something else about the jungle. It can be an intoxicant. When the sun and the humidity and the insect count fall, one's spirits rise correspondingly. Conditions outside the body come to terms with conditions inside the body. A physiological-psychological balance is reached, and the beauty of the forest is revealed.

In Whitehill's case, there were, of course, contributing factors. He was exhausted, hungry, lost, and he had just witnessed the murder of one of his kidnappers. Nonetheless, his endorphins had kicked in, and he was profoundly, blubberingly happy. He began to find green soothing and the occasional shaft of sunlight a wonderful surprise. He became aware of new smells that his limited olfactory vocabulary could label only as varying degrees of musky. The pounding progress of his feet connected him to it all, and he was content to be part of the growing, flying, slithering, swimming, running, stalking, crawling life that shifted about the jungle floor and breathed each other in and ran past the Indian and...

"Hey, Whitehill. You OK, man?"

Aterarana was behind him.

"Sure. Yeah. I'm OK."

"I was waiting for you, and you ran right by me."

"Oh, well, I was…I saw you. I was getting ready to stop."

"C'mon. We'll rest a second."

"All right. Rest time."

"You better sit. How do your legs feel?"

"My legs? Fine, fine."

A far-off squawk cut through the forest above them. "Macaw," said Aterarana. He watched Whitehill closely, measuring the glaze in his eyes, the beginning of a drool on his lower lip, the dirt and the bugs mingling unchallenged on his face. "OK. We've only got a couple hundred yards to go, but it's straight uphill."

"Why uphill?"

"We settle on top of steep hills so any potential attackers will be tired and lose any element of surprise by the time they get to us."

Whitehill looked up. He could not see past the second layer of leaves, where branches of neighboring trees began to intertwine, but it was enough to gauge the angle of ascent.

"Yep, that's steep."

"One more thing. No one should get this far without being detected, so you should have quite a reception party on top. Frankly, I'm not even sure what to expect. Nothing to worry about. Just say and do as little as possible."

Whitehill had not considered what he might find when they reached their destination. Aterarana had supplied no details, and the issue had been suspended while he concentrated on the jungle. It had all been difficult to absorb. He found it difficult to believe he was where he was.

But his thoughts were catching up to him. Now White-hill was worried. Now he wanted to be back in Pittsburgh.

"If you really feel all right," said Aterarana, "I'll lead. If not, just tell me and I'll hang behind to catch you if you fall."

"No, I'm all right," Whitehill lied. "How do you get things up there?"

"We don't need very much. There's firewood and the garden produce, which the women bring. And the men carry whatever game they catch. All of that can be tied on our backs. The building material, trees and stuff, was already up there."

"Oh."

"And we have a stream running down from a little higher up the mountain. Fresh, clean, cool."

"That sounds good," Whitehill replied without looking up. He squashed some mud under his boot and watched it ooze out the patterns in his soles. Whitehill noticed he was doing a lot of that lately. Doing stupid little things and noticing he was doing them. Now he was noticing that he was noticing that he was doing them.

"Whitehill?"

"Yes?"

"All set? It's OK. You'll be a hit. Once the women see those pants, you'll be the most sought-after guy in the village."

"OK. I'm OK. Let's move 'em out."

There was another macaw, calling sharply, behind them this time. Aterarana smiled at Whitehill. "Indian," he said, and started up the trail.

A Guest in the Jungle

* * *

Whitehill fought to maintain control of his adventure. The elegantly constructed detachment that had allowed him to endure the fatigue, the swelter, and the bugs of prey was crumbling. He watched himself make that terrible leap from objectivity, and when he landed inside himself—when he realized with frightful clarity that he was the star of this jungle movie, that he had been living in constant danger, that he was walking into a tribe of Amazon Indians—he shut down.

The jungle closed in around him. As Whitehill climbed, he watched only his hands alternating before his eyes, one grabbing for support or balance, one pushing off. They were the same hands Whitehill had used to manipulate silverware, write legal briefs, count out change, and explore what he believed to be erotic areas of young women's bodies. He had caught baseballs and footballs with them, dressed with them, turned book pages, driven, cooked. He'd seen them at work over the years gesturing, punching, caressing, grasping. He was longingly remembering his hands in elementary school, folded obediently on a desk, the anticipation of mischief tingling his palms. But now there were more hands, reaching for him, pulling him to his feet, and helping him up the hill.

Whitehill knew these hands belonged to the Indians, and he was powerless to stop them from dragging him out of second grade, right back into the Amazon jungle. He was led through a webwork of red-brown arms and dark eyes into an enormous room. Someone eased him into a hammock. Cool water was splashed over his forehead. Aterarana materialized at his shoulder and handed him warm, smoky strips of meat.

Beyond those gathered at his hammock, thatched walls sloped and disappeared dimly above. An opening far across the room let in the afternoon sun, which blinked as it caught soft, gliding silhouettes. Whitehill guessed this place to be oval-shaped, at least two hundred feet long, its height way out of proportion to the tapered ends. The actual boundaries were obscured by a number of other hammocks strung around the perimeter, by the smoke from embers now being persuaded to flame along a center line, and by the curious faces of those who occasionally bent over him. It felt like Halloween.

"Whitehill," said Aterarana, "this is the chief. Chief, Whitehill."

The man was an arm and a face, indistinguishable from the rest. Incredibly, he wanted to shake hands. Aterarana handed Whitehill a large gourd of water.

"Mr. Whitehill," the chief said, "the Lotimone welcome you to our home. You may treat it like your own."

Whitehill studied the chief's lips. Yes, he was quite sure he could understand the words coming out. "Thank you."

"I have asked that you be left alone at first, though we are all quite curious about you. That one from the outside has come so far. An accomplishment, Mr. Whitehill. You are the first in over two hundred years."

The chief nodded to Aterarana, smiled at Whitehill. "Be seeing you." A man of few words.

"OK, Whitehill," Aterarana picked up. "How you doing?"

"That's difficult to say."

"Listen, I tossed a few things into the water here. It should relax you."

"Oh no. Not again. And I don't need to be any more relaxed. The way I feel I may spend the rest of my life in this hammock." Whitehill made a determined face. "And I've gotta know what's going on. I'm tired of getting knocked around this jungle like a pinball."

"Whitehill, you are so out of it now that you're only half-awake anyway. You're probably going to forget anything I tell you, and I'm just going to have to tell you again."

Whitehill clung defiantly to his gourd, stubbornly refusing to drink.

"OK, Whitehill. The reason Lotimone Indians speak English, among other languages, is that we have had some contact with your civilization even though 'civilization' has had no contact with us. How's that?"

"Well, that's better."

"Better? Only better? You're a hard man, Whitehill. As of right now, you are the only person alive that knows this other than the Lotimone ourselves."

Whitehill took in the bare-breasted women bent over cooking fires, clusters of naked children giggling in the shadows, a man to his right shaving the tip of an arrow. "What good does it do you to speak other languages?"

"Good? Well that is a matter of constant debate. But it's a fact that no commerce is conducted in Lotimone, no college courses are taught in Lotimone, no..."

"College!"

"You have something against college?"

"As a matter of fact, I do, but that's beside the point. What do you mean, college?"

"I mean a group of buildings that fancies itself an institution of higher learning."

"Yeah. Well, we're talking about the same thing, but why are we talking about it? I mean, here?"

"The Lotimone have got this intellectually ambitious streak. Half the people here have been to college."

Smells from the dinner fires began to smother those of the forest. A community of tree frogs bounced their evening greetings off the hillside. Whitehill looked across the room and took a deep breath. His mouth made the shape necessary for a word, but no sound came out.

"All right, Whitehill. Let me give you the whole thing. A couple of hundred years ago, a missionary stumbled into our territory. We were based about fifty miles southwest of here then. We shot him before he ever got close, of course, but he didn't die. He dragged himself after the men who shot him all the way back to one of our villages. The tribe was sufficiently amused, and they threw him into a corner of some hut until they could figure out what to do with him. So, he hung on, begged enough food to stay alive, and eventually recovered.

"The tribe never accepted the guy, but he learned our language and with some kind of crazed, religious determination managed to convince a few men to return to civilization with him. They checked it out, and when the missionary leaned on them a little too hard, they came back. All but two.

"After a couple of years," Aterarana went on, "the temptation to make another excursion into the outside world proved too great. A second group came out and found the first two guys, who by now had some kind of life going.

A place to stay anyway, and a little money coming in. And that's how it all started. Since the early seventeen hundreds, members of our tribe have been slipping in and out of the jungle. Some never go. Some go and return. Some don't return. If you knew where to look, you could find Lotimone all over the world. No one but a Lotimone knows where to look, however, because no one outside of this jungle knows we exist. Except you."

"Why?"

"When you live in the middle of a jungle, a secret can keep itself. But mainly because those who remain like their lives uncontaminated, and they guard their privacy. If the world ever found out about us, it wouldn't take long to destroy our life here. And this is a very rich area. Clearly, that must be concealed from the outside. Oil, diamonds, uranium, gold, too. That's how we finance most of our tribe who live in your world. All of whom, by the way, must have false identities because they are not citizens of anywhere. There are a lot of technical illegalities."

"What about emeralds?"

"Yeah, we've got emeralds, too. Not so many, though. Why?"

"I'll tell you in a minute."

"Anyhow, we give most of it away. There's a small foundation we run in midtown Manhattan. Medical research, mainly. It's the only thing the whole tribe could agree on."

"Medical research!"

"We gave a lot to develop the polio vaccine. Into kidney transplants after that."

"Kidneys?"

"A doctor in Cleveland turned us in that direction."

"Cleveland?"

"Yeah, I used to go there a lot to talk to this kidney man and watch my favorite baseball team," Aterarana replied, his voice full of pleasant memories.

Whitehill roused himself. "You go to Cleveland to distribute funds for medical research?"

"Not anymore. And before I came back home, I was trying to steer foundation money into food problems."

"Food?"

"Lot of hungry people, Whitehill, and a famine on the way here in South America. Plus it was time to diversify. It was mostly medicine then, except during World War Two." Aterarana added, "The Lotimone backed you guys."

"You backed us?"

"The French, really. Gave money to the Resistance. Why did you ask about emeralds?"

"That Dr. Darreiro said something about showing me a fortune in emeralds."

"No, doesn't make sense. It's possible, but he'd stumble on that other stuff first. And why would he want to share it with a stranger?" Over Whitehill's shoulder, Aterarana caught the chief's eye. "Did he mention anything else?"

"Plants and insects."

"Ha ha. There're enough of those. But there aren't many botanist-kidnapper-entomologists."

Whitehill rewound the events of the last few days. "I didn't believe him, but I couldn't get a handle on whether he was insane, or what." A moment later he asked, "Why did you shoot that Indian he was with? Because he was on your land?"

"Ah, your escort." Aterarana had been deep in meditation. He emerged in a more serious state of mind. "He was a Tsavi. Our tribes have been feuding for generations. They refuse to make peace, so unless we bring in a load of machine guns, we're forced to remain on the defensive and play by their rules. They recently killed one of us. It'd gone unavenged. If a Tsavi had penetrated our territory unchallenged, he would have returned tomorrow with a raiding party."

"Then why don't you bring in machine guns or something?"

"It's tempting, but unless we keep it pure and pristine here, we have nothing. Or, we would soon have nothing as we made compromise after compromise. Where could we draw the line to be sure that our way of life wouldn't be eroded? The glories and evils of the outside world would drag us under pretty quick. Our one exception is a small chest of emergency medical supplies."

"This whole thing is astounding."

"There's a lot more going on in this world than most people are aware, Horatio. Now, I've got to go talk to the chief. I suggest you finish off your drink there. You need the rest."

Whitehill sipped his water thoughtfully. As with most discoveries, the point of acceptance, of letting go, opened into an area of calm. He held onto Aterarana's final word and let it roll on through.

* * *

A high-pitched buzz in his ear. Whitehill had been told there were two kinds. The operational sound of one's central nervous system and, at a slightly lower register, blood zinging through the veins. He had never checked whether this was true.

The hammock held his body evenly, comfortably. He reluctantly opened his eyes and pushed himself upright. The *bohio*, the name Aterarana used to refer to this giant room, was almost deserted. Golden-gray sprays of sunrise leaked through the entranceways. A fresh selection of chirps and whistles, different in character from the evening sounds, mingled with the chatter of women and children. There were few men.

Whitehill was surprised to have fallen asleep so easily, slept so soundly. This was the first morning he had not expected to wake in a hotel room, or in Pennsylvania. Relieving himself in the crisp morning air, he walked around the *bohio*.

The terrain had been cleared in front of what appeared to be the main entrance. Behind him, the mountain rose toward the sky. Long, open slices of bamboo zigzagged from somewhere above, holding a steady stream of water, which they delivered to a sunny area next to a small shelter. Though he had never been one for the outdoors, Whitehill was overcome by the simple elegance around him.

The Lotimone's position on the hilltop opened a view for miles. Tufted green tops of jungle lined the rolling landscape. Slight indentations in the leafy carpet must be the hunting trails; the larger ones, rivers and streams.

Tightly packed clouds rimmed the wide sweep of sky, a soft, bright blue pressed over the mountains and the mountains beyond that and beyond that. The rising sun tinted various sections with turquoise and aquamarine as they fell away toward the pink edges of the horizon. In the nearest valley, the sun was baking last evening's moisture into delicate, low-lying mist. Whitehill followed a bird skimming high over the treetops yet still far below where he stood. Then he realized he was not alone.

A strangely familiar young woman, slightly behind and to one side, wearing only a length of cloth wrapped about the waist. She wore her nakedness without embarrassment under his scrutiny. Her movements were graceful, her slenderness offset by wide, strong shoulders.

The Aero Amazonia stewardess.

Whitehill's "Good morning" popped out more enthusiastically than he had intended.

"Beautiful, isn't it?" she asked.

For an instant, Whitehill thought she was referring to her chest. Recovering self-consciously, he managed a yes.

This was the sort of woman one was accustomed to seeing, but not knowing—a woman glimpsed through the window of European sedans or laughing confidently at someone else's table. She used the fingers of both hands to adjust the strap of a shoulder bag between her breasts, a strap that seemed too roughly woven to be allowed access to such areas. Her lips were rich and full, her eyes dark and set effectively at half-mast.

She smiled, and he continued. "It is beautiful. I mean that. I've always thought about what beauty might be and called things beautiful, like a painting or something, but I know this really is. Not that I was being hypocritical before. I thought I was evaluating it on my own, but I actually was applying it to some standard of what beauty was supposed to be."

"OK."

"OK, what?"

"I know what you mean, but I think you're carrying on a bit. You're uncomfortable because I'm half-naked."

"That's ridiculous."

"Are we disagreeing already?"

"No. I mean yes." Whitehill lowered his eyebrows importantly. "After all I've been through the last couple of days, it's going to take more than a little nudity to shake me up. I've been racing through the jungle, crossing swollen rivers, sidestepping snakes..."

"Hey, I live here. All that's commonplace."

"Oh, I guess it is," Whitehill agreed. "What about kidnapping?"

"Kidnapping is the logical extension of almost every Indian raiding party," she said deliberately. "Especially attractive women."

Whitehill was about to say something sarcastic, but he was not sure of his cultural footing, and he chose not to risk insult. She sat down, and the soft tan cloth opened above a knee, revealing most of one thigh. Whitehill remained standing. "Where are all the men?"

"Hunting."

"Yeah?"

"They leave early, drift in before midday, and, if necessary, head out again when it cools down some in the late afternoon. Have you had anything to eat?"

"No, I'm pretty hungry."

"You ought to be. You've been asleep for two days."

"Two days!" It seemed incredible that he was being pushed through such extremes.

"That's what they tell me. I just came in late last night myself."

She produced a package of leaves and a pair of small bananas, all still warm from the fire. Whitehill mashed the sweet fruit on the roof of his mouth and swallowed without chewing. The package contained the same type of meat he had eaten on his arrival.

"This is delicious," he said between mouthfuls. "What is it?"

"Smoked tapir."

"Ah hah."

"Do you know what a tapir is?"

"Tapir, no."

"It's sort of half pig, half horse. They go a couple hundred pounds."

"Dangerous?" Whitehill was quick to spot any new candidate for the list of threats to his existence.

"Not really. It's fairly tame because a lot of tribes consider it one of the incarnations of the god of rivers and rain, so they leave it alone. The only danger comes because it's so dumb and clumsy."

"I don't get it."

She grinned in a way Whitehill found ingenuously cute and stretched back against the slope of hill. "When a tapir is rattled, it'll head for the water, fast. It's big enough to mow down anybody or anything in its path, including a canoe if it's tied up where he jumps in."

"Do you believe it to be the incarnation of the god of rivers?"

"They don't teach that at Radcliffe."

"Then what do you believe?" Whitehill was not sure how he was performing in her eyes. Was that a foolish thing to ask? He realized that in this new environment, his thought processes had fewer guideposts.

She seemed equally uncertain and looked at Whitehill strangely. "I used to believe in the goodness of human nature. They didn't teach that either. Not in practice anyway; maybe in intent. But that's mainly why I'm here and not there, which is what you were getting around to asking me."

"What?"

"What do you mean, 'what'?"

"I think I have a right to know what I was getting around to asking you."

"You want to understand why I choose to live in the jungle instead of a city."

"I should want to know why any of you do, but it makes a crazy kind of sense to me now that I'm here," Whitehill reflected. "It's easier to believe you would take this life of simple values and beauty over traffic jams than it is to believe you people exist in the first place. But here you are."

"The amazing part is here *you* are."

"What I want to know is how you got from here to Radcliffe."

"When I was very young, I was taken from the jungle to live in Lima. I learned a little English in school and later moved in with an uncle in Miami. Et cetera, et cetera. To get to Boston from here I would go the same way you would, with the possible exception that I always take trains over planes when I can."

"What about Aterarana?"

"My kid brother. We were together in Peru and in Miami, but he chose to go to New Orleans for college. He said he loved the city's sense of humor, which certainly couldn't be said about Cambridge." She stood without using her hands and took Whitehill by the arm. "C'mon, I'll show you a place you can clean up, and then we'll take a look at that cut of yours."

Whitehill allowed himself to be led over a narrow path that wound along the mountain. When the jungle tightened, they were forced to walk single file. His hostess's high cheekbones were echoed in the upward arch of her loins.

"What's your name?" Whitehill asked.

She turned. A flush came to her face from beneath the layers of tan. "Avritalana," she replied, "but Avri is enough." Whitehill could not remember ever having taken a hike through the woods with a half-naked woman, an oversight he now regretted.

"Chauvinist response," Whitehill mused to himself. "But then again, perfectly natural, biological."

They had entered a shady grove. Two miniature waterfalls emptied into a clear pool. Avri slipped out of her wrap and dived in. "Ah well," he sighed, "it doesn't really matter."

He stripped slowly, pausing to brood in fascination over the welts and slices under his clothes. At one point he had to tear his shirt away from an encrusted strip of blood where Bakiratare had cut into his hip.

At last Whitehill stood naked in the jungle. He felt foolish without his clothes, wanting to appear just the opposite but unable to stop himself from guessing what venomous surprises might be lurking beneath the water's surface.

"Say," he began, as nonchalantly as circumstances would permit, "are you sure this is safe?"

"It's fine. Just jump in. Don't wade."

Whitehill executed a timid surface dive, one that minimized his penetration. He emerged beside Avri, her hair sleek and glistening behind the ears. She was striking.

The water worked its instant magic on Whitehill, cleansing, cooling, calming. Even so, as he began to tread and paddle about, the image of his toes as ten tiny, dangling bait shrimp refused to go away. Still, resting his feet on the bottom was out of the question. If there was a bottom.

"What was wrong with wading?" he asked.

"Oh, sometimes rays hang out at the shoreline," she said smartly. "The sand covers them, and they're tough to see. Before you walk in, you really ought to poke around with a stick."

"Rays?"

"Stingrays. If you step on them, they sting you."

"I thought you said it was safe."

"Well, it's pretty safe."

Whitehill was already wearied by keeping track of notions that resisted correlation with anything else in his brain.

"OK. Let me get this straight. It's all right to swim in a pool with stingrays as long as you don't step on one going in."

"That's right."

"How do we get out?"

"We just have to be careful. By diving in, we already cut our chances of being stung in half."

"Great, great. For a moment there, I thought I was enjoying myself."

"Relax."

"Oh, I have relaxed. I've figured how to get out safely."

"How?"

"Behind you." Whitehill dipped his head in the water and flicked the hair off his forehead.

"What a guy."

"How about snakes? We got any snakes here?"

Avri floated on her back. "Yes, but you'd practically have to land on one directly to make it mad. All this thrashing about scares them away, anyway."

"Anacondas?" Whitehill had seen a few jungle movies.

"Yes, but the big water boas are slow, and they usually swim on the surface, so you'd see them if they were there…and as far as electric eels go," she continued, warming to her role, "they usually don't find their way in here. Good thing, too. They get up to eight feet and as big around as my thigh. Very territorial. They'll attack anything."

Whitehill waited until he was sure Avri was watching and then disappeared beneath the water, feet together. He stroked twice while staying under as long as he could, coming up in the center of the pool.

"You're not scared at all, are you?" Avri called.

"The truth?" He dived again and grabbed her arm when he came up. They bobbed in the water inches apart.

"You know, Whitehill, as little as ten years ago, you would have been shot entering our territory, just like that Tsavi."

"Why?"

"Actually, the situation never came up because no outsider ever got this far. But if one had, if you had, we would have killed you immediately."

"But why?"

"Because the tribes that resisted were the only ones that remained Indians. Those that gave in became niggers, third-class citizens."

"So what changed ten years ago?"

"We faced the inevitable. We saw the jungle shrinking in on us. Colonists, missionaries, prospectors, oil companies, government agencies, farmers. We realized that killing one wouldn't stop the others. It was beyond our control." Avri slowed her pace, narrowing her eyes ever so slightly.

"We had tried to stop it," she continued. "For instance, in Lomalito we had our agents buy land and business interests to slow it down and got a brief reprieve when it stopped growing. As a matter of fact, that's why I took the Aero Amazonia job. I became one in a long line of monitors. It was just to take a close inside look at how developed these jungle towns were getting. But there are too many other factors. The fact that you made it here, regardless of how, is a signal that our protective buffer is in jeopardy. We've had to give up."

"I'm sorry."

"Oh, don't be. You're very lucky. You're going to see the last of the last. Standing on the spot marked X. The sun setting on the American Indian." She brushed his hair back at the temples. "Of course, I should warn you that certain members of the tribe are not so resigned and may present a problem for you."

"Problem? For me?"

"Last night while you were asleep we had a meeting to decide what to do with you. Aterarana carries a lot of weight, and it was his decision to bring you in, so you really didn't have that much to worry about. You should be flattered how few people wanted to murder you."

"Murder!"

Avri splashed a small wave into Whitehill's open mouth. "The chief seemed to like you. The shaman's got no objections. And most importantly, we need you to confirm our suspicions about who this Dr. Darreiro might be and why he was on his way into the Tsavi. Be glad you're with us and not them."

"No argument."

"Let's go dry off."

True to his word, Whitehill followed her footsteps right onto the bank. Avri turned to him, her mouth slightly open, her hands on his waist. They faced each other, dripping wet. She drew her arms along his side, working up to massage the back of his neck, fingering the gash line of Bakiratare's strikes.

It struck Whitehill that there was no more appealing quality in a woman than relaxation. A distant but insistent twinge reminded him of Monica, his girlfriend, a woman unable to move through life without the silent reinforcement of *Women's Wear Daily*, unable to move through the rooms of her own apartment without stops at strategically placed mirrors.

But here was Avri—natural, at ease. Whitehill could not believe his luck. He welcomed the stirrings of desire, a rush of tense muscles. He watched her eyes as she stepped closer, almost touching now, her breasts nearly brushing his chest as she bent down, trailing her fingers lightly along the back of each leg. Her warmth pressed through the gloss of moisture from their swim.

Whitehill felt as though he'd suddenly been forced to look down from a great height. He shuddered slightly, balanced his hands on her shoulders. Avri reached into the mud, swung a dripping scoop up to Whitehill's hip. She stood, lightly slapping a second glop over the wound at the side of his head.

"What...?"

"Got to keep out the parasites."

Avri took him by the hand a short way into the forest. "Papaya," she said, breaking one open. "To speed the healing."

It occurred to Whitehill, who only seconds before had believed himself to be on the threshold of some universal, cross-cultural discovery, that perhaps he knew even less about things than he had imagined.

Avri worked the fruit pulp into Whitehill's side and then, more carefully, into the cut behind his ear. Completing the operation, she grabbed him behind the neck and briefly pulled their lips together.

"You'll be fine," she said, and slipped off through the trees.

NINE

The next few days moved tranquilly for Whitehill. Though not all in the tribe were reconciled to his presence, he was formally accepted as their guest and treated as such. He turned out of his hammock with the rest, long before sunrise. The Lotimone ate in family groups, each unit gathered around one of a number of small fires. His spot was between Aterarana and the chief who, as Whitehill was not surprised to learn, were father and son. Avri tended the coals. A dozen assorted aunts, uncles, and offspring completed the circle.

There was something agreeable about these cool, quiet times, before every move became an effort. Breakfast was usually yucca and leftover game from the previous dinner. Smells were strongest in the morning, sour and smoky. They heightened Whitehill's perception of where he was. His sense of distance—not only of place, but also of time and custom—inflated the smallest details with importance. He became acutely aware of the jumble of weapons, utensils, and personal garments hanging from the rafters, the changing quality of the clay drying into a pot, the way thin twine fastened arrowheads to a reed shaft—blunt, rounded tips for birds, a shard of bone for fish, and long, sharpened triangles for bigger animals.

The food was dull and, most often, unspiced. Whitehill, however, found it so exotic that he was able to eat only small amounts. With so many distractions, he was less careful to tend to his body, which grew lean and dark left on its own.

Aterarana and Avri had taken him out after his first full day of consciousness, and once he could walk around relatively unafraid without worrying about where he would spend the night, how he would find his way out, or who was chasing him or kidnapping him, his senses opened.

He watched for snakes now as a matter of color and shadow, not fear. He saw the rise and fall of rivers, and felt the increased savageness of mosquitoes as certain sections dried. Stillness broken with a crash was a falling limb; a sudden cry meant some animal had been unexpectedly seized. He noted that the rich, florid plants gathered below, ferns soared above, palms stood alone, lianas twisted everywhere, and certain orchids attached themselves to tree trunks. Aterarana showed him which of these might hold two or three ounces of clear water in the early morning.

Avri acquainted Whitehill with the local geography. Trees and turns in the hunting trails that had seemed indistinguishable now shaped into landmarks. Whitehill was pleased to discover that many of his fantasies about how the jungle must look were accurate.

The accumulation of soil and sweat usually made it necessary to end each day's lesson with a swim, a practice that strained Whitehill beyond frustration. They lay by the pool, Avri stretched on top of her unfolded waistcloth, and

Whitehill settled into the spongy earth, his head resting on a neatly folded rectangle of Brooks Brothers pants. Nudity was insignificant here—as was this business of lying next to a beautiful, unclothed woman, skin outdoor-taut and rounded with intriguing dimples where her body adjusted to various postures.

Whitehill seemed incapable of shrinking the few inches between them. He dug deeply into his store of romantic memory and technique, a maze of dimly lit passages where blurred images of Errol Flynn and Humphrey Bogart squired expensive women through exotic possibilities; where Whitehill himself flailed away on pullout couches, living room floors, and springy Sealy Posturepedics. But whenever he managed to bring the conversation down to the two of them, here, now, Avri effortlessly launched into less intimate arenas.

"I'll tell you something," she said. "It's very hard, in your land, if you're not the favored group of the system. White, and male, too. You have to use up all your best energy saying, 'I'm black, I'm a Hispanic, I'm a woman, and I'm just as good.' If you don't do that, the system sucks you under; if you do, all your creative juices have been used up just getting even."

"Things are getting better, but I see your point."

Whitehill briefly considered the advisability of bouncing a papaya off her head to get her attention. He elected instead to swim, diving between cool green shadows, eyes open, stroking to loosen the muscles in his back. Avri remained on the beach and was waiting for him as he emerged. He wiped water from his eyes; she stepped toward him. Something was happening. Her body moved into place, her breath shorter than it should have been.

The sexual charge Whitehill had tried to lose in the water again seemed to be zapping between them, but he couldn't be sure. She rocked slightly on her toes, her breasts tilting in response. With difficulty, Whitehill held himself in. He would be an enthusiastic player, but was there going to be a game? There was the problem of his hands. Something would have to be done with them soon. Avri was standing in one place for a long time. She wasn't going for the mud though. That seemed a good sign.

Whitehill found himself skimming the length of her thigh, grabbing, pulling the rounded curves of her ass.

Avri slid her arms around Whitehill's waist, squeezed, and lifted him into the air.

Locking one leg behind his knee, she threw him to the ground and scrambled on top. Avri planted her knees in a straddling position and grabbed for Whitehill's wrists. He tried to sit, but she pushed him away.

Whitehill looked up, saw her intent on securing a hold, and began to fight back. He twisted underneath, but she rode him and kept fast. Finally he worked a hand free, caught her above the hips, and shoved.

They fell kicking to their sides, struggling for control. Turning noiselessly in the sand, she strained into him, but Whitehill held and with a shoulder drove Avri onto her back.

He flung his weight over her. Avri wrapped hard legs around his as they found each other. Whitehill thrust inside, and she angled up to take him, groaning whispered phrases from an unknown place. They became a raw, natural lust so complete that Whitehill forgot to worry about the chances of rolling over a poisonous spider. Kissing deeply, each dropped into an overheated, rhythmic frenzy. He grabbed the two halves of her and rushed through in spurts and spasms.

After a time, the jungle returned. Whitehill spun slowly onto his back. "Was that the usual courtship?"

Avri laughed softly, drew it out into a hum. "I guess it's the savage in me."

Whitehill glanced over quickly to confirm that this was a joke. He was adrift in an unfamiliar world but, at the moment, content enough to take a step back. A huge weight disengaged from his chest and hovered in the trees. "I feel," Whitehill said aloud, "as though I've somehow been missing the point."

"You mean about sex?"

"Well, no, not sex." Whitehill balanced on an elbow. "It's like I've been running alongside a train and just jumped on."

"I like that, the train part."

"Thank you. Want to hear the rest?"

"What I want is the Sunday *New York Times* and a cigarette."

"Knowing you as well as I do, I take that to mean yes."

"I guess," said Avri, "I'm going to get it no matter what."

Whitehill grinned. "I feel immune to sarcasm."

A large fish rose from the water with a snort. Avri laced her hands behind her head, raised a leg, and rubbed it over Whitehill's waist. Dark leaves rearranged the sunlight into drifting, silky green shadows.

"Anyway," he went on, "I know I've been in an incredible rut."

"And now you're not?"

Whitehill shifted to full release. He had passed into a state of mind heretofore unknown in far reaches of the Amazon Basin. "I used to get incredibly upset watching television."

"What?"

"Eyes filling up with tears, throat getting thick, all that. First it happened watching an old newsreel of American troops liberating Paris. Then it was the six o'clock news, then old movies."

"Why?"

"Well, I'm not exactly sure why. Something to do with being touched by the forces of good and evil, or by simple kindness, or sometimes injustice. Then I couldn't help evaluating the quality of my life and I guess everyone else's. And television. I had a front row seat for tragedies halfway around the world, and I was privy to intimate details in the lives of soap opera characters who never existed, but I didn't know fuck-all about my next-door neighbors."

"Television can do that."

"And cable. One hundred channels and TV banking, TV shopping, TV college, TV church, TV computers, TV video games. Pretty soon people will never have to leave the house."

Two families of spider monkeys swung in the branches overhead. Whitehill sat up. "But that's why you're all here, isn't it?"

"Pretty much."

"Do you know I used to buy boxes with pictures of chicken or peas instead of buying chicken or peas?"

"Why would you want to buy peas in the first place?" Whitehill looked offended. "I'm sorry," continued Avri, "but you jump into things so fast, no preliminaries."

"I could say the same about you."

Avri reached behind his neck and kissed Whitehill gently on the forehead. "Yes. Well, go on. I didn't mean to stop you, only get you focused, slow you down."

"I just feel kind of crazy here. Free, really. Like all bets are off. Culturally, that is. Nobody looking over my shoulder. And even though I don't know anything about living in the jungle, it seems like I have more real control over what happens to me. Know what I mean?"

"More or less."

"A couple of months before I left the States," Whitehill went on, "I stopped in a restaurant with a friend of mine. In the last year we'd probably been there twenty times. Anyhow, the waitress took our order and then came back in two minutes and said, 'That will be $12.90.' We told her we hadn't gotten our food yet, but she said she couldn't serve us unless she got the money first. So I said, 'What's going on? I come in here all the time, and I've never had to pay before I eat,' And she says, 'Manager's orders.'

"I asked to see the manager. He came over and said, 'You're the same two guys who were in here last night and ran out without paying.'"

Avri chewed a blade of grass. As she listened to Whitehill, a soft, sudden wave of emotion passed inside. Something not sexual, warmer, more like the feeling that prompts everyone to pet the enthusiastic family sheepdog. She smiled indulgently. Whitehill rambled on.

"We kept saying, 'No, you have us mixed up with somebody else,' but he wouldn't budge. I invited him to sit down, and we talked. I pointed out how stupid it would be to come back the very next day if we had run out on a check the night before, but he said he was sure it was us.

"Finally I said, 'If this were a murder trial and you were an eyewitness and the verdict hinged on your testimony, would you positively identify us as the two guys who did it?' and he said, 'Yes, positively it was you.'"

"You were making him defensive," said Avri.

"Probably, but how could I not?" Whitehill brought himself back. "Did I tell you I'm an attorney?"

"Nope."

"In any case, I began to sense this guy at a completely different level. He was out of sync. It was like he was struggling to get back, and the effort he needed to hold on to his position was causing something to decompose under his shirt. There was kind of a sweet metallic odor coming up from his collar. I watched him trying to realign himself with the flow of things.

"I was mad—and frightened. Everybody seemed to be making up their own, selfish versions of reality to defend their own little abstract territory. Sometimes they didn't even believe what they said, but once they'd said it, they had to defend it. They'd do anything, just so their own rationalized view of life could survive, and that seemed to be what practicing law was about, too."

"I know," returned Avri. "It's a jungle out there."

"I didn't know where the world that I was supposed to live in was. Why, I used to… What did you say?"

"Never mind," said Avri. "Enough about what I think. Let's talk about you for a while."

When Whitehill stopped laughing, it was only because Avri had managed to place her lips over his. He was beginning to have a very good time.

*　*　*

As the days passed, Whitehill sought bolder rewards from the jungle. He was invited on the hunt but could survive only the morning or the afternoon excursion, never both. The hunting paths were barely discernible, used only for access to deep parts of the forest. Generally, they pursued game across whatever terrain the animal's trail led. Deep sections of the wilderness were so choked with vegetation that fifty yards of penetration meant an hour-long wrestling match with the environment. Whitehill invariably returned exhausted and empty-handed, muttering about how a work-out with the New York Giants would have been easier. But he had come under the spell of the rain forest.

At first, he had been disappointed. On the hunt, the Indians seemed to behave no differently from anyone else. He envied their ability to slip naked through the jungle, especially when he was encumbered by several pounds of water held in his clothes after crossing a river, or when his shirt caught while sliding under a low bough or between two trees. And, of course, they went about their business with a lot less thrashing and general all-around noisemaking than he did. But they didn't really seem to be acting like Indians until two hours into his first hunt, when Aterarana stopped him with one hand on his chest and the other on his mouth.

He pointed into the distance. At the farthest limit of his vision, Whitehill could discern a black speck of a bird flitting in the treetops. Aterarana stood framed in the leaves, silently fixing a blunt-pointed arrow in his bow.

He plucked a leaf off a nearby plant, placed it over his tongue, and made a noise that Whitehill realized was identical to the one coming from the direction of the bird. The two called back and forth, the quarry drawing ever closer. When the bird slipped into range, it cocked its head curiously and leapt less often from branch to branch. Aterarana waited for a clear shot. Minutes later, the bird was hanging from a sling on his back.

Whitehill had not handled a bow and arrow since qualifying for his Junior Brave pin one summer afternoon at Camp Pa-hu Cat-a-Wa. The requirement for this award was hitting the target. When it became apparent that his aptitude in this area had not improved with age, Aterarana taught him to use a blowgun.

The chief selected a venerable old weapon about eight feet long. Aterarana showed Whitehill how to wrap cotton around the curare-tipped darts for a snug fit in the shaft, how to aim it like a rifle by sighting down the barrel, how not to inhale.

A blowgun is used only on small animals, since the muscle-relaxing effects of the curare take too long on larger game. Whitehill was given a set of piranha jaws for scoring the darts used to kill monkeys. If a wounded monkey attempted to remove one of these darts, it broke in half and the poisoned end remained inside.

Aterarana was able to hit a golf ball–size pod of fruit a hundred feet off. With practice, Whitehill was able to hit a considerably larger banana at close range. There is always more than one way to prove your mettle, however.

At the end of a steamy afternoon, Whitehill was following Aterarana home from a disappointing hunt. Aterarana had one scrawny bird on his sling. Whitehill, for his part, was experimenting with the best ways to carry an eight-foot pole through a dense rain forest. He shifted his blowgun over one shoulder, hands opposed and about three-fourths of the way down the shaft.

It came from above the opposite shoulder, a jaguar in full pounce off Aterarana's blind side. Whitehill swung instinctively, landing a respectable home-run blow between the eyes of the cat. It dropped heavily, snarling short of its mark. Aterarana spun and sent an arrow into the stunned animal's heart.

Whitehill's legs trembled, but he thought it was with excitement. "Is it dead?"

"Pretty close," said Aterarana. "I don't think I've ever seen that done before."

Whitehill touched a flank. "It's beautiful, huh?"

"Female. Very unusual to attack two humans. Must have a young cub to feed."

"Oh."

"So now you're sad?"

"Couldn't we go look for the cub?"

"What would you do with it, and," Aterarana said, sweeping out one hand, "where would you look?"

Whitehill pondered that.

"This is what the jungle's about," said Aterarana. "Death is an intimate affair."

"Yeah."

"Anyway, you're the one who hit it on the head and made it mad."

Whitehill had his moment of fame at the evening meal as he recounted the adventure. Avri rewarded him with a succulent portion of roasted wild turkey, and the tribe listened kindly as he expanded on the phenomenon of hunting in general and the circuitous, unnatural procedures imposed on most animals en route to the dinner plate or paper carryout bag.

Those afternoons not devoted to the hunt were spent poolside, stretched out alongside Avri in slightly less athletic duplications of their first amorous afternoon.

Within Whitehill, a deep certainty was beginning to emerge. Once popped out of the womb, one continually bumps into others of the same circumstance like so many billiard balls, and once set in motion, one can never hold on to a permanent course or state of mind any more than one can rest in the fleeting instant of the present. Avri may have known all this and she may not have, but she certainly acted as if she did.

"Look," she said as he listened enthusiastically, "somebody like you comes across new information every day. You're always going to be changing your opinion. Or at least enough to keep an open mind on the fuzzy issues—the universe, the meaning of existence. If you spend too much time thinking about life, you're not altogether in it. Relax."

And he would until the evening meal, when he was always asked to recall what he could of Dr. Darreiro and Bakiratare. Much of the discussion was carried on in Lotimone, but Whitehill assumed this was for speed and convenience and took no offense. That Dr. Darreiro had made contact with the Tsavi was certainly a matter of concern, but the fact that he had penetrated Lotimone territory, even unknowingly, was the main topic of discussion.

Both women and men took part in these nightly conferences. Whitehill surmised that men hunting while women tended to food, children, and clothing was simply the most efficient way to distribute the work. The Lotimone, in fact, appeared to be so egalitarian that one could live with them for months and never figure out which one was chief.

But one was, and it was he who patiently explained the Amazon's particular problems to Whitehill. The chief was a small, agile man with close-cropped white hair. He seemed pleased to speak English, choosing his words thoughtfully and surrounding them with broad gestures. When they sat by the fire, Whitehill fixed himself a long, sharpened stick and roasted bananas as though they were hot dogs. "The worst of it, Whitehill, is slash and burn."

"Sounds very urban."

"Oh, no. Quite different. This comes out of a feeling of national insecurity, something akin to the idea of Manifest Destiny you had in North America. It compels all the countries around here to send in settlers so that they can conquer and secure their frontier territories. Naturally, they ignore the boundaries of any lands titled to Indians.

"These colonists must clear the land to farm it," he went on. "In other words, they cut the jungle down and burn it up. A couple of years later, they discover the soil has no nutrient value left, so they abandon it and cut another swath. The land that's deserted needs hundreds or thousands of years to regenerate. Consequently, this jungle is disappearing daily, kilometer by kilometer. Even if we utilize all your Western technology, less than one percent of the Amazon can sustain agriculture, yet governments and international banks keep pushing these pioneers in.

"There's no real population control, and there's not going to be any way to feed everybody. The prospects in South America are horrible. Moreover, since a symbiotic relationship exists between this jungle and an incredible amount of rainfall, when this greenery goes it's going to alter climatic conditions throughout the globe. There's never been a wide-scale annihilation of plant species like there has with animals."

"But these are the biggest plants I've ever seen," said Whitehill. "How could they get like that if there aren't many nutrients in the soil?"

"Ah, it's only the strong that survived. And they have to be large to compete for sun and water. Even so, it's astounding how quickly any forest can vanish." The chief made a brief calculation in the air. "Half the forests in the world have been destroyed in the last thirty years, and the jungles probably won't last the next forty."

Whitehill stretched his legs, massaging the places that had stiffened. The chief picked up a blowgun dart and twirled it between his fingers.

"Our immediate concern," he said, "is that when the jungle shrinks, the animals disappear, and with them, our way of life."

"Well, I thought there were people helping the Indians. These pro-indigenous organizations down here, and missionaries."

"Some of these groups are well-meaning," replied the chief. "Our experience has been that even the knowledge-able ones become caught in bureaucratic tangles and the corruption that seems inherent in third world politics. Even among the best there's still stealing and skimming off the top when the actual money and goods are delivered. We try it occasionally ourselves, organizing tribes, teaching them their rights.

"But the missionaries?" the chief went on. "Well-meaning, certainly. I might have been too hasty, though, when I said slash and burn was our biggest problem."

"Go on."

"Typically, when a missionary can make contact with a tribe, the first thing he does is learn their language. Over the next months, he'll figure a way to write it down and teach the Indians to read."

"That doesn't appear to be so bad."

"Uh-huh. Amazing in its way. Only a fanatic could do it. All this time now, since the missionary hasn't been run off or run through, he's constantly been doing the most extraordinary things. Producing strange music from a small box, fire from an even smaller one. Wearing exotic woven cloth, giving away machetes, mirrors, beads, crayons, and rifles. He proves to be a powerful medicine man."

"OK."

"In the face of all this, the Indians reason this man must really know about everything. They feel anything they can do, the missionary can do better. He's forced inferiority on them. When they've learned to read, the first book he gives them is the Bible. By that time, after all his lectures about how their view of things is wrong and his way of understanding is the only way, they're so ensnared and overwhelmed they don't have a chance. They become passionate over whatever religion it is that this man happens to endorse. Why, they don't even believe there are other options... I hope I'm not offending you, Whitehill. Are you a religious man?"

"Me, no. Well, I don't know. I'm not even sure all this isn't just an illusion."

Aterarana raised himself from the depths of a nearby hammock. "If you believe everything is just an illusion, White-hill, why do you worry so much about stepping on a snake?"

"Because," Whitehill returned, "the snake might not know he's just an illusion."

"Ha, ha," said the chief, "very good, I think."

It seemed to Whitehill that this remark was about to inspire Aterarana. He quickly cut him off. "What about anthropologists? They seem highly motivated."

"Anthropologists?" echoed the chief. "A respectable lot really, for academics. They just can't seem to resist helping the populations they work on. There was one fellow, he's famous now. I can't remember his name, but you'd recognize it. At any rate, he was writing a book about a certain tribe. Not too far from here. A week's march. Maybe ten days.

"He found the evenings were unpleasant because the particular design of their communal house trapped the smoke from cooking fires. The Indians didn't seem to like it much, either. Always rubbing their eyes and smelling like last night's dinner. So, the anthropologist cut a hole in the roof. Worked wonderfully. Let out all the smoke.

"Unfortunately, it happened that for generations the smoke had been keeping away a certain nocturnal insect. Either the reason the house had been constructed in that manner had been forgotten, or their immunity had been lost over the years, or both, because the tribe was wiped out in a matter of weeks."

"That's terrible."

"It was. The smaller the world gets, the harder it is to be left alone." The chief lowered his eyes to etch small star-shaped designs in the loose soil.

Aterarana flipped out of his hammock and joined them by the fire. "Don't take that personally, Whitehill."

The chief looked up. "By no means. I apologize, Whitehill, if that's what you thought I meant. We've all enjoyed your visit." He sighed. "Things have been breaking down here lately. With the jungle closing in around us, there's more competition for the land, and the Tsavi are growing bolder. Not long ago they crossed the river, surprised one of our hunters, and murdered him. For the first time, they didn't even attempt to hide the evidence. They left him right on the trail."

Whitehill turned to Aterarana. "That's why you killed Bakiratare."

"Exactly. Vendetta."

"It's fortunate for us," continued the chief, "that through your escape we were able to learn about the presence of this Darreiro person. This is quite serious."

"It's likely he's hooked up with some oil or mineral company," said Aterarana.

"We are fairly certain of this," said the chief. "We don't know what they are up to, but it's not the first time we've suspected their interest in this area. Even now Avri is overdue in Bogotá to spy, you might say, on our most likely future enemies."

"Give her a call when you get back," said Aterarana. "She's an entirely different person in the city."

Whitehill realized that he had not lately given much thought to his return. He enjoyed feeling at home in the jungle. Now, under the trance of night, the rush of memory and possibilities left him mute. Somewhere, over many dark miles, lay Lomalito, and farther, all his old belongings, still packed and resting in a corner of his parents' attic.

"I don't think there's any immediate danger," the chief went on. "For you, that is. They had plenty of opportunity before. Nonetheless, my son has volunteered to escort you back to civilization. By a very interesting route, I might add. Not the shortest way, but through our allies, the Basibo. To my knowledge, you'll be the first, er, white man in their village."

"To Aterarana's knowledge also," said Avri. She had slipped up behind Whitehill and, arms folded, was leaning into a supporting pole. "He wants to take you into the Basibo because it will make him a big shot to show you off. I think you ought to stay for a while. Till we're sure it's safe."

"It's safe. It's safe," Aterarana replied. "Don't worry about your pal here. I can take care of him."

Avri made an exaggerated face that expressed her doubt. All three turned toward Whitehill.

He tightened his lips a moment, then relaxed into an easy smile. "Yes," he said, "it's right. I wasn't thinking about it at all, but when you mentioned going back, you activated some kind of internal homing device. I'm powerless to turn it off."

"The morning, then?" asked Aterarana.

"All right."

TEN

At the intersection of two twisting alleyways, a lazy nine-iron shot from the quietest plaza in Bogotá, there is a colonial mansion of modest size. The descendants of its original owner, victims of unfortunate political alliances, were forced to sell around the turn of the century and leave the continent. For years it remained vacant, passing from one local real estate agent to another, until a visiting Frenchman purchased the property in 1929. The outside was left untouched, but within he created a restaurant.

In no other place from Panama City to Tierra del Fuego is international cuisine blended so successfully with regional specialties. Antiques of the period lend a quiet elegance, and an unbroken line of red-cheeked, overweight French chefs maintains the uncompromising standards.

No advertisement has ever been run, no sign has ever been erected. A small brass plaque was nailed into the front door in 1947 and remains the only identification. Despite these precautions, lines are sometimes unavoidable, and for this reason regular customers are allowed to enter through the stained-glass double doors off the patio.

A special table in the center of the dining room is reserved for visiting dignitaries, but if none are about by nine o'clock, these same regular customers are allowed to slip in without a reservation. It was here, amidst the bejeweled and financially favored, that a very fat man sat across from a young bearded American dressed in blue jeans.

"Remarkable," said Ryder. "I raise a glass in your honor."

"Hmmm?"

"I don't know why I'm continually amazed at your abilities. I've seen you in action often enough."

McJeffers pushed aside a stack of dishes. He made a mental note to step up the frequency of these occasional forays to civilization in pursuit of wine, women, and restaurants. "You say something?"

"Never mind. Another brandy?"

"Hell, yes. Where's the waiter? Ah, Nando. Dinner was great. It's always great, but aren't your portions getting smaller?"

"No, *señor.*"

"That was a joke, Nando."

"I know, Señor McJeffers. And a good one. But you asked me the same one last night. Do you want me to say again 'the portions aren't smaller, you are getting bigger'?"

"Ha. No, I guess not. Better bring us a whole bottle. Could be a dangerous night."

"Funny thing about this place," said Ryder. "Whenever you leave here, you never seem to be hungry."

McJeffers broke off a section of bread and poked at puddles of rich brown sauce on the closest plate. "OK, so what have you got?"

Ryder spoke softly. "What we've got is this Darreiro guy, who you'd have to guess was scouting out which Indian lands to seize and relaying it back to this Tavars and García."

"That would be pretty hard to stop."

"Damn right. Then you've got old Whitehill who managed to disappear in one day."

"That could have been the *chuchuasco*."

"The stuff's powerful, but it's not going to make him disintegrate."

"No." McJeffers laughed between sips. "What does your little Miss Salcedo think? And what's her first name, anyway?"

"Avri. But she never likes to use it. Strange, huh? Her idea's even stranger."

"Give it to me."

"She seemed to think that Darreiro kidnapped Whitehill, brought him to the Tsavi as a gift."

"For what?"

"Human sacrifice."

McJeffers put down his glass. "Why?"

"To fire 'em up. Start an Indian war. The tribes massacre each other, the land becomes uninhabited, and the geologists move right in."

"There are easier ways."

"They're getting tougher to get away with. Too obvious. Too many do-gooders watching what happens to people screwed by the multinationals. A journalist could make his reputation for life if he caught up with a story like that: 'Standard Petroleum Slaughters Primitive Tribes to Steal Their Land.' This way, it would look like natural causes, if anyone even noticed."

"So, what are we supposed to do? Stop an Indian war?"

"Hell, I don't know. How often do you get a chance to stop a war? She's got other ideas. It might be something more drastic than that." Ryder poured himself another Cognac. "Anyway, some foundation in New York keeps calling, but they'll speak only to her. When she gets back to town, maybe we'll be able to piece it together."

Despite his best efforts to the contrary, McJeffers found himself increasingly interested in the whole affair. He knew from experience that the more excited Ryder became over a project, the more likely they'd both be to find themselves dangling from the dangerous end of some risky predicament. He ran a massive finger around the rim of his snifter. "Human sacrifice...you know very much about the Tsavi? It seems to me...uhm...there's something I heard, but I can't remember."

"Well, I know that if Darreiro's throwing some Western magic on them, tape recorders or Polaroids or anything, they're going to look on him as a medicine man, which means they won't dare refuse his wishes. He might have pulled off a massacre without Whitehill."

"How does their sacrifice come in?"

"It's tied up with the sun, I think. Most ancient religions believed the sun was the greatest part of creation. They worship it. When you live in the equatorial jungle, running around in the shadows all day, you can really feel the sun's power when you enter a clearing and it blasts you in the eyes."

"You're telling me."

"If the sun's going to have strength and give strength, it's got to be fed. They figure it's the heaviest thing in the cosmos, so they give it the most sacred food they have—human blood. I think they feed it with fire, too," Ryder said. "I've seen Indians shoot flaming arrows at the sun."

"I've seen villages where they cut off the heads of their prisoners, stick 'em on a pole, and let 'em stand guard."

"Yeah, they usually believe once they've killed anybody, they can turn the spirit's power to their advantage. I guess the only reason you got out of there was they didn't have a pole strong enough to support a head that size."

"Ha ha," said McJeffers. "I don't know about that. There're also Indians that will strip off the victim's skin and pick some tribal big deal to wear the bloody thing and pretend he's the god the guy was sacrificed to. They never give me any trouble because there's never anybody around big enough to fill my shoes—er, feet."

Nando approached, balancing a delicate tray. "From Chef Marcel. A present."

McJeffers's eyebrows raised. "I don't believe it. Chocolate chip cookies."

"Still warm."

Nando smiled. "This is very American, sí?"

"Very American. Um. Tell Marcel please, the food was so good tonight we may even pay our bill," said Ryder. "Thanks, Nando."

"Did I ever tell you," munched McJeffers, "about the tribe that makes cookies out of dried yucca and strips of human flesh?"

Ryder tossed down a half-eaten cookie as McJeffers attacked the rest unopposed. The room had cleared. Nando opened both patio doors onto the night sky, admitting moist garden breezes. Joking waiters methodically stacked chairs in the corners.

"So what do you think?" asked McJeffers.

"I think you never had anything to worry about. The reason all those tribes spared you was that the victim's usually a person of great honor."

"I give up." McJeffers folded his hands over his stomach. "I'm getting kinda tired in my old age."

"Now, Whitehill, on the other hand, had blond hair, didn't he? Like the sun. It's always best if the victim fits the image of the god. Maybe they could just cut his hair off and somehow possess its strength."

"Nope. They'd still have to kill him. Fear of retaliation."

"Yeah," replied Ryder. "I guess. If they're an aggressive bunch, once they've seen some blood spilled, that's all it should take."

"I just remembered, the Tsavi do sacrifice," McJeffers said. "They used to, anyway. There's a sort of gladiator ceremony with some dances and mock battles. Then they take their fiercest warrior and give him a special club with a lot of sharp blades in it."

"Then?"

"Then they bring on whoever the victim is and give him a club the same size but made entirely out of feathers."

Ryder stared into his glass, playing with the tides. McJeffers ate cookies. The check was presented, and Nando sighed as he received his customary twenty percent tip backed only by a signature. He helped Ryder hoist McJeffers out of his chair and walked them into the evening. "*Adios, señores.*"

They lumbered up the alley toward a wide, flower-lined boulevard flanking the square. Ryder flipped a silver coin in the air. "Feathers?"

"Better than nothing," said McJeffers. "He's probably still OK. Nobody's heard anything about Indian trouble." He began to whistle.

"Um hm." Ryder scanned the patterns of stars hanging over the general direction of the Amazon. "My guess is Whitehill's in a lot of trouble right about now."

ELEVEN

"Look, Whitehill," said Avri. "Let's not make a big deal out of this. Don't worry about it. I'm cool. You're cool. No long good-byes." She shook his hand and sauntered off into the sunrise. "Stay in there, Whitehill."

Whitehill watched her go. "OK."

She stopped on a small rise, a darkening shadow set against the pale peach sky of jungle morning. "That's it?"

"Well, you didn't leave me much room."

"Sorry." Avri turned, the light deftly catching her profile. She tucked a wandering spray of dark hair behind her ear.

"It's just unlikely that we'll ever see each other again," said Whitehill, "and I want to let you know my life's probably going to seem very dull for a while."

"It goes both ways."

Whitehill shyly inspected the toes of his boots, warming to the moment. "I…" he began, but Avri had disappeared. Aterarana emerged, grinning, from behind a convenient shadow.

"Jeez, what a beautiful moment. I loved the way you handled that. Don't think I'll ever forget it."

From within the receding limits of night came a sound that Whitehill realized he'd unconsciously been waiting to hear ever since his plane first touched down in Lomalito: "Ku-wa, ku-wa, ku-wa, eu-eu-eu-eu-eu." It was the one mandatory birdcall on every jungle movie soundtrack.

"Aterarana, what is that?"

"C'mon, Whitehill. I don't know everything. It's a bird."

"I have a feeling," Whitehill said, "this is going to be a tough trip back."

"In the jungle, every journey begins with…"

"I know. The first step."

"No, breakfast. Let's go. They're all waiting for you."

* * *

Most of the tribe had put off their morning routines to join Whitehill in a farewell meal. Choice gobs of parrot flesh and sputtering hunks of reheated armadillo were handed to him, but he had little appetite now for even these.

As they settled before the burning glow of an extravagant breakfast fire, Whitehill was unexpectedly seized with a paralyzing, overwhelming comprehension of where he was. The moment had changed. Things decelerated, time suspending to the point of unavoidable self-awareness. Nothing had happened, but he felt panic quicken his heartbeat and weight each breath.

Uncertainty jumped from everywhere—the movement of someone's hand, someone's eyes, the angle of a stick in the flames, drops of fat from the meat, all tightened around him in a slow dance of piercing chaos. If life could unbalance this way, it was out of the question. A fear of nothing burst inside, then hit a pocket of reserve. He toughed it out and surfaced.

In an instant, it was clear—the change in diet, change in sleeping habits, the stress of the jungle, of stepping back in time, of being the focus of an Indian tribe's attention, the kidnapping. Whitehill reawakened to the group, heard their easy jokes. No one seemed to have noticed. He exchanged smiles with the chief. His subconscious had been holding all this in check until it was time to leave. And it really was time to leave.

Whitehill relaxed and exhaled with passion. He trembled a bit as they stood, but the worst was far behind. Handshakes all around and an embrace from the chief, who slipped a string of jaguar claws around Whitehill's neck.

"The one I hit?"

"Yes, only warriors ever earn these."

"Here we go." Aterarana tapped his shoulder.

Whitehill waved, a grand one, flapping over his head as he ran after Aterarana. Down the hill, on his way home. He felt reinvigorated, composing, humming tunes to the rhythm of his boots slapping the jungle mud.

Aterarana waited at the bottom until Whitehill caught up. They hooked off into one of the main hunting trails, jogging at a good clip. A slashing rainstorm had whipped through the night before. The trunks of trees along their path felt blood-warm and moist, alive.

They plunged through dark, verdant shadows that obscured the mysterious twists and turns ahead. Down the slope of a yellowish patch of woods, the trail merged into a shallow creek. Their progress was recorded in gentle splashes as they hit smooth stones underneath, plopping along the water's course. Vines, branches, and stalks closed the foliage into a cool and quiet roof overhead.

The tops of Whitehill's shredded socks drooped heavy with water. He stopped to rip off an inconvenient piece that sported a miniature cloth alligator hanging by a stitch. He liberated the beast, placing it carefully on the surface of the creek to watch it drift downstream.

Whitehill the warrior grew increasingly satisfied with himself. His experiences now began to assume heroic proportions. Intrepid adventurer. Certainly that was how he'd appear to the folks back home. Triumphant return. They'd identify him with the jungle. A soaring spirit that tested his power against the elements. Breaking free from the diurnal humdrum of life in a way that could not fail to inspire his dullest admirers.

He imagined narrating this very moment at a cocktail party, the living room suddenly hushed: "Next morning, this Indian and I struck out into the bush. Good fellow. He'd given me a few pointers with the blowgun. At any rate, as a token of his esteem, the chief had presented me a set of jaguar claws. Well, not esteem really. They were from the same jaguar that I..."

"Whitehill."

"Hmmm. What?"

"Want to rest a second?" Aterarana rubbed the sole of one foot.

"Rest? How long have we been going?"

"Two hours maybe."

"Really? I'm not even that tired."

"Your endurance has improved. Go rest in that hut while I find some fruit."

"Hut? O-ho-K."

Aterarana counted off the seconds it would take for
Whitehill's eyes to adjust to the light inside.

"Five, six…"

"Yaah—shit!"

Aterarana rushed in. A scarlet skeleton swayed over the
far corner. Whitehill pressed against a wall on the opposite
end.

"What the hell is that?"

"Wait. Quiet." Aterarana delicately picked up the bones
of a limp wrist and pressed his ear to the rib cage. "It's all
right. I think it's dead."

"Of course it's dead. What's it doing here?"

"I'm sorry." Aterarana made no effort to suppress his
chuckle. "I couldn't resist." He handed Whitehill a tough-
skinned green and orange fruit he'd started to peel and
began to work on one of his own. "You don't want to stay in
here, do you? It's a funeral parlor."

Aterarana had already turned to go. He ducked as the
fruit flew past and calmly handed Whitehill another. "Last
one. They're pretty sweet."

Whitehill found he could not sulk and eat at the same
time. He fell in step, somewhat less intrepidly. "OK, tell me."

"We're not in Lotimone country anymore," said
Aterarana. "The Indians hereabouts take their dead to the
river and leave them for piranha. After a while, the skeleton
is removed, stained with the urucu plant, and hung in these
huts."

"Why?"

"That's their business. Never asked, but I'm sure they've
got their reasons."

Whitehill sucked the last bit of juice from the fruit and sailed its seed into the leaves. "There aren't piranha in all these rivers, are there?"

"Yeah, but their legendary ferocity as man-eaters is much exaggerated," Aterarana replied. "They can do everything they're supposed to, and I've seen them make the water boil, but piranha naturally go after other fish, and there are plenty of those."

Whitehill sighed. "So we don't worry about piranha."

"Not unless food gets scarce. Like, if the water's low enough to cut off a channel somewhere. The kandiroo is the one you ought to be concerned about."

"What's that?"

Aterarana raised an eyebrow. "You mean Avri never told you about the kandiroo?"

"No."

He laughed. "It's a kind of worm-parasite. Lean as nothing, maybe half or three-quarters of an inch long. Likes to swim up any available body opening and wedge itself in with barbs. Very painful. Nothing short of surgery will get one out."

"Umh."

"The moral of that story is be careful where you go skinny dipping."

Now that he was finally on his way back to civilization, Whitehill realized how local his concerns had become. Which insects might be harmful to him, which animals might contribute to the tribe's food supply. This fruit was edible; that plant could heal an infection. Instead of deciding what to buy in a grocery store, he'd learned which arrows to use on which game. Instead of puzzling out the best routes through rush-hour traffic, he'd been memorizing trails.

"We're coming to a particularly magical part of the Amazon," said Aterarana. "There are spirits all around us here." He had walked through a curtain of trees to the edge of a narrow red rock. It jutted horizontally from the side of a steep hill to hang dangerously over the valley they approached. Whitehill crawled out after him.

Aterarana pointed to a waterfall that seemed to pour from an outcropping of stone in the clouds. It began as a wave, surging through a coppery swath that split the crest of a towering jungle wall. The great height strung the cascade into mist and spray before it reached the bottom. "A lot of the world used to look like this, you know." He spotted a pair of large hawks circling and bouncing in the hot air currents above the trees. "That's where we're going."

"This is great." Whitehill might have spoken many minutes on the greatness and grandeur of the moment, but something Aterarana had said disturbed him. "Say, Aterarana, do you really believe…wait, that's stupid. I mean, what did you mean about spirits?"

"I figured you'd respond to that." Aterarana grinned. "Don't get too excited." He stepped back to the trail and continued. "I'm not permitted to talk about some of it, but I can definitely say there are noises here, absolutely inexplicable sounds that I haven't heard anywhere else in the jungle."

"Like what?"

"Like bagpipes. Like bluegrass banjo. Like someone laughing for hours. Like giant pieces of metal that keep crashing together. Like something I can only describe as the hysterical howl of a wild French poodle."

"The howl of a wild French poodle?"

"Um hm."

"And this is where we're going?"

"Ah, you're going to have a fine time. You're turning into a regular Jungle Jim."

"You know," Whitehill began again, "I know what you mean." The path had opened some, and as he made his way behind Aterarana, he was able to use his hands while he talked. "I do feel more connected here."

"That's it. Most aspects of civilization take you farther from what's essential."

"Is that it?"

"No." Aterarana was growing Whitehillian at the sound of his own voice. "It's now that you have a choice of two perspectives, two different worlds, you can see things more clearly."

"Yes, but…"

"From here you can see that civilization has advanced to where a man or woman just shuffles paper all day. They begin to confuse the labels of things with the things themselves. It's built in. Stockbrokers, insurance agents, all those businesspeople working with paper that has only indirect relation to its meaning."

"I know, but…"

"Then you've got doctors and lawyers, no offense, rising disproportionately to the top on other people's misfortunes. And don't even talk to me about the advertising business."

"I won't do that," said Whitehill.

"And," Aterarana went on, "they all march along unconsciously, following the steps of a system they've come to believe is the world, drawing esteem from their meaningless, artificial level over those below, courting approval from those above. Acting like people they see in the movies instead of like themselves...it's like prolonging adolescence through your whole life." He plucked off a slender leaf and tore it apart as they walked. "You're all removed. You exist in a maze of artifice and posturing. That's why your society spawns so many psychologists."

"And comedians," Whitehill put in.

"Ha. Comedians, too. That's right." He put a hand on Whitehill's shoulder. "So what do you think about all that?"

"I think," Whitehill said, "you sound like me."

Aterarana laughed. "Wait a second. I might have been ranting a bit, but I couldn't have sounded that confused."

"Consumed, then."

Aterarana fell silent as he considered this, and they quickened their pace for a while. Whitehill trotted behind, observing how his friend was able to slip through improbable, suffocating tangles without disturbing a leaf. He tried to picture Aterarana with the other world's trappings—Aterarana in an apartment, a taxi, Aterarana waiting in line at the dry cleaner's, ordering in a Chinese restaurant, holding a briefcase, a golf club, a parking ticket, a calculator.

"OK. That's enough. I am starting to sound like you. Whenever I get close to this spot, I always think about that stuff." Aterarana marked off a number of paces from a pile of rocks on the forest floor, pulled out his machete, and cut an opening between some palm trees.

Whitehill followed for a few yards until Aterarana stopped and began slashing in all directions. This was no path-making, but haphazard, vicious slices left and right. There seemed to be no purpose to this madness, but then the answer came to Whitehill all at once. He was staring at the rusting remains of an airplane. Aterarana had cleared off part of a wing, the length of one side, and was working into the cockpit.

"Don't know anything about it," Aterarana panted, anticipating Whitehill's question. "It's looked like this since the first time anyone found it. No bodies."

The smell of fresh-cut grass now hung thickly over the wreckage. Whitehill stepped to the window on the pilot's side. He was dissuaded from sticking his head in by a family of huge cockroaches that spilled out of the ceiling.

"Interesting, huh?" Aterarana perched on the tail. "There's a tribe you'll meet not far from this spot, but they're not the kind that could have given much help. Anyway, the noise of the crash probably kept them away from here for months, if they were even aware of it."

Whitehill took an almost proprietary interest in this artifact from the outside world. He walked completely around the fuselage, pushing his boot against certain points in the manner of one appraising a used car. Something in the sweep of the plane's design gave him the feeling it belonged to people of great wealth. The circumstances that delivered it to this place cried out for drama, romance, adventure. "What do you think happened to them?"

"There is a legend…" Aterarana began.

"I knew it." Whitehill tensed his imagination.

"…that the only survivor was a young boy, adopted and raised by a family of great apes. He learned to talk with animals, swing on vines…"

"All right. Shut up."

They ate a brief meal on the airplane wing, and with the assurance of more remarkable things to come, White-hill set off in an inspired state of renewed enthusiasm. But the scene had had its effect on him. He longed to feel a sidewalk's predictability underfoot, to order whatever he wanted in a restaurant, to come across somebody he'd recognize from the past, to be cold enough to wear a sweater. The scent of rotting wood was in the air; wet leaves slapped his face. Although it remained hidden, he knew they were passing close to the waterfall.

When the jungle finally thinned, Whitehill could see they were traversing an odd set of jagged hills above the falls. Immediately in their path, a giant boulder rose from the mist. It was anchored in a circle of very regular granite blocks. From where he stood, the boulder presented an imposing outline that looked remarkably like a man with a hat. He turned questioningly to Aterarana.

"Whitehill, I'm going to have to extract a second promise from you."

"What was promise number one?"

"Promise number one I hope is understood. Not to supply any jeopardizing details about your stay with the Lotimone."

"Of course."

"Number two is never, in some future fit of archeological necessity, reveal the location of the lost city."

"The lost city?"

"OK. Maybe not ever. I really don't care much about the lost city. We just want to keep people out of here as long as possible. Once they get a look at this, the tour buses wouldn't be far behind."

"What lost city?"

Aterarana assumed a jaunty air. "The one you're standing in." He led Whitehill closer to the granite rocks. At this distance, strange carvings emerged from the shadows. A parade of wild, bug-eyed jungle animals laced around flowing, geometric symbols.

"This is fantastic. What is it doing out here?"

"I told you. Relatively speaking, it's not out anywhere. It's in the middle of a city."

"So where is this city?"

"All around us. What's not underground is overgrown." Aterarana cut a hole in a nearby mound. Using the machete to carve more than hack, he cleared the dirt away from what became a flat stone wall.

Whitehill rubbed his hand in the opening. "Just fantastic."

"Predates the Incas, we think." He pulled Whitehill after him. "Now you've got to meet the mole people."

"Wait a minute. Wait a minute." Whitehill planted himself against a rock. "The mole people?"

"Mole people. They live in the ruins. Underground caves. It's possible they're descendants of the original inhabitants, but more likely, they just took the place over."

"Mole people, though."

"Yes. That's not what they call themselves, but you'll see. We ought to find them before it starts to rain."

"How do you know it's going to rain?"

"It rains every day here about this time. Unchanging climatic conditions." Aterarana turned his face into the cool, hazy wind that had begun to blow. As he did so, the leaves behind them stirred and a twig popped. "Here's a guy now. Mole man!"

Out of the leaves he heard, "EEEEE. Moman, moman."

"I'm the only one who calls them that," said Aterarana. "Mole man!"

Whitehill stared at the spot from where "moman, moman" seemed to be coming. Aterarana opened his small pack and unwrapped a cloth that contained hard, sharpened lengths of bamboo.

"Moman." The voice grew excited. Aterarana offered his gift, blade backward, toward the sound.

The mole man crawled out of his camouflage. He was covered more by hair than by skin. The hand that reached for the knife was long; the fingers, short. "Moman" scurried back under the protection of the leaves. Though much taller, he had never risen more than three feet from the ground.

"See," said Aterarana. "Mole man. Nothing to worry about."

"My god. How did he get like that?"

"Probably, he's just never gotten beyond that. I think that was us not long ago."

"God."

"That's another question altogether. Let's go. It should be OK for us to come inside now." Aterarana gave Whitehill the remaining two bamboo knives to hold. They ducked into the place through which the mole man had disappeared, bending to fit down a low opening through the bushes. The path grew steadily darker until it widened at the end before the entrance to a large cave. The eyes of a mob blinked from the gloom.

Aterarana grabbed Whitehill's wrist and shoved his arm into the mouth of the cave. The gifts were grabbed quickly, but politely, from his hand. "Moman. Moman. Moman. Moman. Moman."

"Told you," said Aterarana. "You're a hit."

Whitehill followed him inside. Conscious of many shapes scuttling about in the dim light, he steadied himself and drew close to Aterarana. Some of the mole men appeared to have tails.

Long ago, all sides of the corridor and entranceway had been cut and smoothed to right angles. The cave turned a corner where a square hole the size of a mail van opened onto a clearing. Outside, the sky changed from silver to gray, the lowest levels of rolling clouds shading quickly with moisture.

The heavens cracked, ushering in a hard sweep of rain. Two mole men raced out into the clearing, a third and fourth screaming behind. As the rest of the cave dwellers swarmed in the doorway to watch, Whitehill was relieved to see the tails belonged to monkeys that loudly made themselves at home with the mole people.

Another mole man ran from the cave to join the others, who by now were on their way back. The thunderstorm raged malevolently. When the mole men reached their audience, they reversed ground again. Two made for the trees, swinging up to torment the low branches; three grabbed fallen limbs, which they whipped around threateningly. Whistling curtains of rain swirled over them. The mole men ran back to the cave, then once more to the tree, which received a sound thrashing with sticks. They all threw back their heads, twisting in circles, stomping their feet, yowling at the green, wrinkled bolts of lightning dissolving in the darkness.

Each returned in his own time. Seconds after the last mole man came through the entranceway, the storm stopped, pushed aside by nightfall. Aterarana motioned to Whitehill, and they crossed over to the main fire.

"Enjoy that?" he asked.

Whitehill squatted next to him. "I've never seen anything like it."

"I think they've got this thing about rain," returned Aterarana, toasting his hands.

"They did seem to react rather strongly, didn't they?" Whitehill could not restrain his laugh. The end-of-the-day fatigue was on him. He let the hypnotic effects of the fire pass inside, but he was not yet beyond the reach of curiosity. "How are they advanced enough to make these fires?"

"I've never seen them do it, but they do go to a lot of trouble not to let the ones they have die out. Oh, and keep this space to sleep tonight if you want to stay warm."

"You know, this room might have been a part of a palace once," Whitehill reflected. "It's only a big hole in the mountains to these guys."

"Yep. The mole people are left alone because they have nothing. I'm one of the few who even hunts in these parts." Aterarana fell back on his elbows. The mole men were futilely pushing around intruding puddles of water with wet dead leaves. "But be careful about passing judgment on them. You're in for a difficult night if you do."

A mole man joined them at the fire. He grunted affably at Aterarana while poking around to waken the flames. Like the others, the mole man wore a small, flat nose and wide lips over a chin of noble proportions. A prizefighter's protruding brow guarded soft, brown eyes.

"No matter what you may see," said Aterarana, "remember we're their guests."

Whitehill thought these didactic warnings unnecessary. Not that he was such a jungle veteran, but he certainly had trained himself to be a good guest. And the fact that the mole people possessed unsettlingly powerful arms and shoulders in no way detracted from his efforts at politeness. Besides, he liked them.

They liked him. A nursing mother, baby at her breast, slumped down right next to Whitehill. The child appeared to be no less than four or five years old, but a good guest does not evaluate the customs of his hosts. When the woman gently nudged the child off and began to suckle a young monkey, Whitehill raised an eyebrow at Aterarana, and nothing more.

"Is this it?" he thought. "Is this the moment when I am finally as far away from home as it is possible to be?" There was something so stupendous, so romantic about this notion that Whitehill allowed himself one of those interior journeys of which he was so fond. Could the thoughts of Columbus, of Marco Polo, have been much different? True, if something should happen to Aterarana, he'd be in for a rough time. OK, an extremely rough time, but—and he was sure of this—it wouldn't be hopeless. No matter what now, he would always have a shot, and that was enough for anybody.

"Hey, Whitehill, I think they're getting ready to prepare us a little dinner."

"Great. What do mole people eat?"

"Mainly these monkeys."

"They do?"

"Um hm."

"But why?"

"They're terrible hunters. They leave that weird mole man scent of theirs on everything they rub against. Monkeys know they're coming a mile away. And even if they manage to kill one, it usually will hang on with its tail, and the mole men have to climb a tree to get it. And they're terrible climbers. So they raise 'em. They eat 'em. And they worship 'em."

If Whitehill had a choice, he would rather not have witnessed dinner preparations. The good-natured mole man who had been stoking the fire seized a monkey from its playgroup. He clamped his hand over one ankle, whirled the monkey overhead, and calmly bashed its brains against the cave wall. Moments later, the scene was repeated.

A mole woman dunked the corpses in a tub of water, gutted them, and tied the tails to a stout beam that hung over the fire. She ripped open both stomachs, squeezing their mess into a crude wooden bowl. An equal amount of water was splashed in, and the mixture was passed around and consumed enthusiastically. Whitehill declined while coughing melodramatically. He pointed to his throat, indicating he had a momentary problem in that region.

Several mole men slipped up behind Whitehill. Elbowing him in the ribs and directing his attention to the upcoming meal, they made noises that sounded like a happy case of collective asthma. Whitehill grinned broadly, tried to imitate the sounds, and then pretended there was something wrong with his boot. This, however, was not such a good idea, since the mole men wished to help their new friend remove the curious, offending object.

Whitehill gave a pleasant neigh which, along with appropriate hand gestures, he hoped would communicate he had things under control boot-wise. As he scanned the assistant cobblers to gauge his success, he noticed that the monkeys frizzling over the fire were not at all still. Yes, they were definitely moving their arms and legs. When one vainly gripped the air with its hands, Whitehill urgently whispered, "They're not dead!"

"They are. It's the muscles reacting to the heat."

"You sure?"

"Yes."

"They're smiling." The skin had tightened in their cheeks, pulling the lips back from butter-yellow teeth in horrible, maniacal expressions of pleasure. Some mole men slapped Whitehill on the back and took the monkeys down. Brandishing their new bamboo knives, they hastily shaved off the charred hair, chunked the little animals apart, and threw the pieces in boiling water.

Whitehill had eaten monkey before, but he paled at the smell trapped in the cave. "Why don't these other monkeys just run away?"

"Fascination with the executioner."

"No way."

"Sure, they're dumb. They've forgotten how to be in the jungle. All their needs are met, and they believe their fate is irrevocable." Aterarana paused to reflect on the creatures. "An evolutionary quirk or two, and the situation might be reversed." He smiled and waved at the cooks who tended the fire. "It's not much different from buying steak. The mole men just live in their slaughterhouse."

"There's still something wrong here. Almost cannibalistic."

"It's only a step away from a farmer feeding a pig or chicken the day before he kills it for supper. Two steps from your dear old aunt buying it at the butcher's. Three steps from you cooking it as a frozen dinner. Four steps from…"

"All right. I get it."

A mole man placed a banana leaf with steaming lumps of meat in front of the two travelers. Whitehill put himself on automatic pilot and ate.

"It's a lot like steak," said Aterarana. "Red, tough. I'm telling you, there's not an eyelash of difference between these guys and the Oak Room at the Plaza Hotel."

"There's plenty of difference."

"It's all in how you look at things," Aterarana continued. "For instance, the mole men don't like to be caught outside at night. Makes sense, right? So, if they're running late, on their way home they stop in a spot where they can see the sun, align it with some tree in their line of sight, and scratch the place where it hits the bark. That way, they think they capture the sun for a while and slow it down. Lengthen the day."

"But that's ridiculous."

"Yeah? Explain to me how it's any different than prayer."

Whitehill never had a chance to reply. A mole man slugged him in the shoulder and pulled his sleeve. Others were excitedly darting about in a dark corner. "Do they want us to follow?"

"That's all I can figure," said Aterarana.

The two stood and were drawn into blackness. "Hey, Aterarana. What the hell's happening? I can't see a thing."

"I don't know. Better get your head down to their level."

The mole men yanked on their wrists. "Shhhh."

"What does that mean?"

"It means be quiet."

"Shhhh."

The passage ran downhill and then flattened. Whitehill was towed by the arm. He raised his free hand protectively in front. They stopped; the air freshened. He was lifted and lowered into a large pit next to Aterarana. They were looking up at the jungle.

It was a quiet place where the woods opened over a river. From where Whitehill lay, he could see a trail following the bank, darkness, and then stars and most of the moon above the treetops. And around a bend, flickering lights. "What is…?" A hairy hand clamped over Whitehill's mouth.

The lights came closer, bouncing in the blackness, throwing sharp, sudden shadows behind the leaves. It was several men.

Whitehill could tell that the angles hid him and his friends perfectly from those on the trail. The mole man's hand smelled strongly of monkey grease. Whitehill carefully pried off two mole man fingers and, as softly as possible, hazarded, "Who…?" The hand tightened again.

The lights were almost over them. It was Indians, armed and moving slowly. Whitehill could hear their jabber. The lead man was probing the path with a bow. The rest, five, had small lanterns, and one was wearing an oversized miner's helmet. Dr. Darreiro.

Whitehill squirmed. He was unable to restrain himself. Out of the corner of his mouth he whispered, "Dat's Dr. Darreiro."

The mole man who was supposed to be keeping Whitehill quiet began to shake. Choppy little snorts escaped from his nose. "What's wrong with him?"

"I think he's giggling."

Another mole man began to snicker, and the man behind quickly put a hand over his mouth. The two looked at each other, and both started tittering like drunks in the front row at the opera. Aterarana began a laugh. Whitehill threw his hands across to smother him and wound up slapping Aterarana in the cheek. Someone faintly exploded at this.

"Shhhh."

They were so close together that anyone's attempt to muffle his laughter rippled through the group in a chain reaction. Whitehill was in school, the teacher's back turned. He buried his face in grass, bit the inside of his cheeks. The mole men doubled up convulsively, each shushing or making desperate, stifling noises that only proved to be hilarious to the others. One broke off and ran back into the passageway. His guffaws echoed through the jungle.

The Indians halted immediately. Whitehill's party froze. He could hear Dr. Darreiro's voice in a volley of concerned whispers. Lights were turned their way. Footsteps. Whitehill was certain he was breathing too loudly. He felt the monkey meat jackknifing in his stomach. For long moments, nothing happened. Dr. Darreiro gave an impatient order, and his group fell back into their march.

No one in the pit moved. The forest was silent. Minutes passed. A mole man picked up his head, testing the air. He banged his fist conclusively on the ground, and the tension dropped.

"Um," said Whitehill. "I thought we'd bought the farm that time."

"If that means get caught, me too."

The mole men chatted merrily and led them back to the warmth of the fires. They were sheepishly greeted by the fellow whose laughter had almost given them away; the look on his face was enough to get them all started again. For the rest of the evening, the mole men took turns saying, "Shhhh." It never failed to get a roaring response.

Whitehill chuckled and shook his head. That he could have been so giddy under the very nose of danger. "What do you suppose they thought all our noises were?" he asked.

"Spirits."

"Ah, right."

"Did you get the feeling they were looking for you?"

"Sure did. But they were going the opposite way, weren't they?"

"Yeah," Aterarana confirmed. "That's the way back to their own territory."

"You know, I still can't figure what he wanted with me." Whitehill hadn't reexamined that aspect of the whole affair for a while. "Did you get a load of him in that ridiculous helmet? He seems like such a harmless, inept fool, really."

"Whitehill, the more decent the man, the harder it is for him to believe in evil."

"Does that mean I'm naïve or noble? No, never mind. I'm falling into a joke, right?"

"Something better. Try this." Aterarana handed him a bowl. "*Chicha.*"

"What's that?"

"You don't want to know. Drink it."

Whitehill, in a rather loose turn of mind, did so. He was soon pleasantly inebriated.

They were facing the fire. Its muted, golden flashes showed the features of the mole people to kind advantage. Fluid shadows softened the backdrop, lowering a cozy intimacy over the giant hole that was at the heart of the lost city in the Andes.

"Aterarana."

"Hmmm?"

"I can't deny I like these guys a lot, but they are still a long way from lunching at the Plaza, or with my dear old aunt for that matter. Or creating a place like this. I don't know whether that's good or bad, but that's what I know."

"Well, make up your mind. It's in your power to advance them several evolutionary jumps all by yourself."

"How?"

"Screw one of the women." Aterarana stretched out on his side, crooked an arm under his head, and closed his eyes. "Your kid'd be main mole man for sure," he muttered.

"Ha!" Whitehill was not sufficiently under the effects of *chicha* to consider this seriously. Of course, he would win himself a permanent place of prestige in mole people history. "Many years ago, an outsider came to us. A man named Whitehill." No. Ridiculous.

A mole guy rocking in the firelight put his hand over his mouth. "Shhhhh." Whitehill fell asleep listening to the ticking of the fire.

TWELVE

His shoulder ached, but he had slept smoothly through the night. Whitehill uncurled from the fetal position. He remembered seeing an oblong cistern in the clearing. Guessing its present purpose correctly, he bathed in the calm of morning. Tentative cries and whistles cut through the thinning fog.

A few delicate drops broke the still waters of the pool. Whitehill was satisfied with his reflection. A little leaner, a little darker, and a lot hairier than the fellow he left in Pennsylvania. Still there, though. Best of all, his image was surrounded from behind by the towering trees of the legendary Amazon.

When he returned to the cave, Whitehill was pleased to find the fire had regained its former strength. His clothes dried before the end of a speedy breakfast. Aterarana and he participated in what he supposed was a soul-stirring farewell for the mole people. It was a blur of physical contact, the chief result of which was that, when Whitehill had said his final good-bye, he found himself once again coated in monkey grease.

Back on the road, Aterarana was in high spirits, warbling an improvised truck driver's song. "C'mon, Whitey, let's make some time."

Morning became afternoon. They stopped in a place where the tops of trees were shaped like huge umbrellas. Aterarana plucked a few bananas and tossed them to Whitehill. "Here you go. So. How did you find your night among the mole men?"

"I loved it."

"Evaluation?"

"As things go on this planet, I'd say they're on the edge of time."

"But not an evolutionary dead end. The mole people are just on their way, I think. They can walk upright. I've seen them do it to get fruit."

"Why get so excited?" Whitehill asked. "According to Avri, once they walk well enough to make their way down to the cities, they'll be lucky to get jobs as maids and busboys. Here they're happy. They certainly laugh enough."

"Damn, Whitehill. You might pass the course."

"Where do we go now?"

"Just the Basibo, and then home for you, boy."

"What are they like?"

"Like everybody else," Aterarana said. "They just want to be left alone to go about their business. Raise their kids. Cook their dinners. Tend their gardens…maybe take some *ayahuasca* once in a while."

"Some…?"

"It's a tea they make from vines. Lets them enter the supernatural." He tossed aside his banana skins and began to walk. "I think that's all I have left to show you."

The path was wide enough to walk two abreast, and Whitehill paced alongside. "Oh, only the supernatural, huh?"

Aterarana raised his arms. "You like all this?"

"I think a lot about air-conditioning, but sure."

"They did a survey once in Brazil. Took a typical hectare. There were almost six hundred full-grown trees. Sixty different kinds." He swallowed his last bite. "You'd never think it could all turn to desert."

"The slash-and-burn stuff?"

"Well that's pretty simplified. What happens is all that clearing the land unlocks it for erosion, which leads to a drier climate."

"Then why isn't that happening in the U.S.?"

"Because the wind pushes most of your water in from the sea. The trees recycle it here."

Their trail opened above. Whitehill walked with his hands in his pockets. He watched Aterarana hoist his bow like a javelin to stretch the muscles in his shoulder. A flock of macaws briefly darkened the sky.

"This way," said Aterarana, indicating with the bow. They began a steep descent. Pairs of green lizards nodded their presence, stupidly electing to scurry to safety only after the travelers had passed.

Whitehill was about to ask Aterarana something when he was struck with a depressing thought. Why was he always asking things? If the situation were reversed, if he were explaining modern life to someone from the rain forest, he wouldn't know anything. He could never reinvent a radio, build a satellite, figure the stress levels on a suspension bridge, describe the manufacturing process for plastic or glass. How does a TV work? You turn it on, right?

He voiced his dissatisfaction with himself to Aterarana, who only kept turning around to look at a place somewhere high above. When he spoke, it was without his usual swagger. "I don't know, Whitehill. Even though it seems like I'm always telling you these things, I don't know. It's like, if you try to pin it down, like what's with the mole people, if you try to capture it in a clear plastic bag, and hold it up and say, 'I got it,' it disappears. And I don't feel very right or have a clear opinion on anything. I could almost as easily take the opposite side." Without knowing it, Aterarana began to walk faster. "OK. There are things I know fairly well. Facts. Jungle stuff. But that's more like I'm tied into these natural cycles, not that I know about them."

A light rain began to fall. It ran down the back of Whitehill's neck, warm, but it made him shiver.

"Lately," Aterarana went on, "I feel like there's some power, somebody out there, outside of things, pulling the strings."

"God?"

"No, not God, I don't think. But it's like somebody is putting words into my mouth, even controlling my actions." Aterarana studied his friend. "It may have been coincidence, but I first got this feeling right around the time I ran into you." He sensed the threshold of a discovery. "You ever feel like that?"

"Yes."

"Go ahead."

Whitehill screwed his face into an expression that allowed him to analyze his memory circuits. "Ever since I got to South America, it seems some outside force has sort of grabbed me by the necktie and keeps yanking me through all these experiences, just letting my chin stay above water... I can't guess what might happen if it decides to let go."

"Hold on!" Aterarana placed his hand on Whitehill's chest and pointed to a spot off the trail. The rains were surely heavy here; most of the leaves hung in strips. There were torn branches, a tree, and beyond that, a step pyramid. Whitehill started forward to investigate, but Aterarana restrained him.

The light, as always, ran uneven and deceptive. It seemed the pyramid was blue and red, iridescent. And it grew; it breathed. A dense, bulging coil six feet high, a solid mass of snake. Inflating, then slowly compressing. Yellow eyes stared from the very top.

"Rainbow boa," said Aterarana quietly. "Aristocracy. The big snakes pretty much get their way on the ground."

"Let's get out of here," said Whitehill without moving.

"It's OK. They're slower than a sloth."

The giant cone expanded.

"Let's get out of here."

"Not easy, is it? These things are hypnotists. They throw a spell over their victim. Paralyze it to the spot."

"I'm convinced," whispered Whitehill, backing up.

"You hear stories about their prey walking right up to them. Can't move. Wait for the body of the snake to wind around their ribs, squeezing just tight enough so they can't fill their lungs." Aterarana picked up a rock. "Ye-hoo!" It thumped off the unconcerned boa.

The shock of the giant snake jerked them back into the moment, interrupting any further cogitations on the question of free will. They picked their way through increasingly lush, wild forest that ran down into swamp. Several times the path became no more than a slender log just above the murk. It was tough mosquito country again. The jungle cries increased in volume; vapors rose from the bog.

* * *

They came upon a section where the overgrown trail lifted them into fresh air. An old man watched them approach. Brown and thinly muscled, he wore a length of heavy-woven, striped cloth tucked into his waist like a bath towel. He howled.

Aterarana howled back and ran to embrace the stranger. They exchanged some words. The old man howled again and bear-hugged Whitehill. He led them across a small stream, up to a stand of high trees. A dozen villagers appeared to greet them. Women wearing the same type of cloth draped over a shoulder; children carrying miniature bows and arrows; men with headbands and tattooed cheeks, some dressed in shirts—the whole group suddenly grew animated. They clustered in a communal area, the old man seeming to conduct the bemused chatter occasioned by the new arrivals.

A row of huts was hemmed in close to the trees, just far enough away to avoid any wayward falling branches. Bright, polychrome birds, hobbled with large sticks, squawked and jumped about the dwellings.

Whitehill was taken into a room where sagging bundles of cotton fiber and baskets of all sizes hung from the walls. Spears, blowguns, and arrows lay in the rafters; firewood and blackened orange pots were stacked neatly on the dirt floor underneath.

The Basibo were very interested in Whitehill, he somewhat less in them. It was all wondrous, but he'd had enough. Now that he was on his way, he very much wanted to go home, to be home. These people fussed over him and seemed all right, peaceful in their way, but Whitehill was growing impatient, irritable. Bored? The outside world had intruded here. The Basibo owned metal pots, muzzle-loading shotguns, steel axheads, even chickens and dogs. Though the tribe was rich by jungle standards, these few items pushed them into a higher league. If the Basibo were entering the twentieth century, they would arrive dirt-poor.

"That may be true," said Aterarana over dinner, "but they don't think very much about owning. When the jungle's your shopping center, the door is always open. Their food, fuel, and shelter are all around them, and it's hard to get rich when the important things are free."

"What about the guns and pots and the chickens?"

"Yeah, they enjoy all that. They just don't like the idea of taking possession. When you have your own things to defend, you've got to back off from the group. Nobody ever does because they like each other and because everyone will tease you if you try to act important. Besides, the group's on the move a lot, following the hunt. You either keep your personal things down to a minimum or leave them behind."

Aterarana readdressed himself to the meal. Then, deciding he was on a roll, he reconsidered and finished his point.

"And they can. Where you hear a noise, an Indian hears dinner. You see mud, they see a bowl. You see a stick, they see an arrow."

"It must be hard," Whitehill said, "for the Indians to understand why the white man goes to so much trouble to clear large tracts of land when it seems more useful left the way it is."

He saw Aterarana raise an appraising eyebrow in his direction, but Whitehill was too busy with the small feast their arrival had inspired to respond. His appetite, in need of rejuvenation, was piqued with helpings of agouti, fish, something that might have been sweet potato, and roasted pig. One of the bowls they kept passing him contained boiled yellow frogs, but this he declined.

Aterarana made the required thank-yous and lay back in his spot at the dinner circle. "Easy, Whitehill. Don't eat too much if you want to take *ayahuasca.*"

"Is tonight drug night?"

"I think probably so. In our honor."

"OK."

"You sure?"

"Yeah. Why? Should I be scared?"

"No, you just seem uncharacteristically rash."

"I guess. Seeing these guys in shirts and the women in plastic beads…"

"It's too soon to begin underestimating. Any time today, if you'd stepped off the trail to take a crap, chances are over-whelming you would have been the first human to ever walk in that spot." As if to underscore Aterarana's point, an unfamiliar, bizarre cry came out of the night. "But you ought to try some," Aterarana continued. "It's probably the only chance you'll get."

"You're taking it, too, aren't you?"

"Um hm."

"What happens?"

"They take it to talk to spirits," said Aterarana, indicating the Basibo. "To learn things, to heal, to get all sorts of valuable instruction and knowledge you can't get any other way."

"But what will it feel like?" At the word *spirits*, Whitehill had sensed the rashness Aterarana spoke of evaporating.

"A trance. A journey through time. You'll fly, see animals, faraway places. Maybe meet your soul."

"You kidding me? Are you sure I'll experience the same things they do?"

"If you have two arms, two legs, five senses, and are predisposed from birth to approach the world like everybody else, sure."

"And it will all be over by morning?"

"By tomorrow afternoon I'll have you in a little settlement with a cafe, a radio, canned corned beef, cold beer, and a half dozen guys competing to fire up their outboards and ferry you back to civilization."

"I'll do it."

"Attaboy."

Whitehill shrugged his shoulders. Aterarana conferred briefly with some Basibo, and amid pleasant murmurs of affirmation, the two excused themselves and walked outside.

"They'll be out in a few minutes," said Aterarana. Whitehill caught his shoulder. A spider, fully ten inches across, lurked in the twilight, its dark body an overinflated purple sausage glistening in the flashes from a cooking fire, muddy hair matting and curling on thick, outstretched legs. "I hate these," Aterarana whispered, handing Whitehill a rock. "Get him. They'll love you for it."

If the spider had turned and charged, Whitehill would have probably spent the night in a place quite far downriver. Even so, the rock squashed its mark.

At the thud, two Basibo emerged from their post-dinner gossip and, after testing the victim with the point of an arrow, voiced their approval. "Bird-eating spider," said Aterarana. They were joined by several more members of the tribe. Each slapped Whitehill on the back in what he judged was the Basibo equivalent of a congratulatory handshake. Flattened, the thing could have straddled an apple pie.

Their group gathered at the stream, where a caldron was emptied and scrubbed. One of the men lit a ragged cigar. Filling and refilling the huge bowl with smoke, he led them all to another building a short distance into the jungle. The pot was handed to a bandy-legged fellow Whitehill had not noticed before. He and Aterarana were seated on woven mats in the circle forming around Bandy-legs. Whitehill could see that this hut had been constructed with more care than the others. Smooth logs were sunk upright in the corners, palm fronds entangled snugly into a roof. But the crossbeams, oddly enough, were irregularly spaced. And every right angle in the room had been obliterated with gentle curves of mud.

"Because," Aterarana explained, "spirits hang out in corners."

The caldron was filled with water and brought to a boil. Bandy-legs, clearly the Basibo shaman, threw in some ants, a tuft of hair, a small fang, three caterpillars, a number of feathers and leaves, a vial of blood, and a toad. "All for show," whispered Aterarana. The circle began a pensive chant. Bandy-legs took some sliced vines from the folds of his shirt. He hammered them politely with the blunt end of a hatchet and, uttering a musical incantation, added them to the mixture.

A bark frieze, stained and sectioned in a checkerboard design, was removed from the wall. Aterarana raised his knees, balanced his elbows lightly on top. "Spirit traps," he pointed. "The pattern confuses them."

Some of the men thumped turtle-shell drums. Whitehill unbuttoned his shirt to the waist. The fire was feverishly hot. Froth seeped over the sides of the caldron.

"You can relax," Aterarana offered. "He's going to let it simmer a while, then it has to cool."

"OK." The waiting was difficult. Occasionally the low conversation and languid drumbeats were broken by noises from the village. A chicken shrieked. A baby cried. The jungle reasserted itself, releasing a mysterious wail that slipped over the drone of Bandy-legs's chant. Whitehill fidgeted. "So, uh, your tribe's been allies with the Basibo for a long time, or what?"

"Yep, pretty long." Aterarana drew out a theatrical pause. "This used to be big rubber country around here. Did you pick up anything about those days?"

"Well, I know everybody refers to it as a boom, and people were trying to turn Manaus into another Paris."

"They had plans for the whole Amazon," said Aterarana. "Furious, scrambling growth and progress. Fantastic fortunes were made. Entire buildings were routinely dismantled and brought in from Europe. Diamonds and gold on every hand. It wasn't unusual to send your shirts off to be pressed in London."

Bandy-legs stirred the foam critically. Satisfied with the concoction underneath, he transferred it into a number of smaller pots using a wide wooden spoon.

"When the automobile tire hit big, the champagne flowed," Aterarana continued. "And greed along with it. There was too much money, too fast. The whole region went insane. Indians were flagrantly enslaved to work the rubber plantations. Their women were raped, their kids thrown around like footballs for fun.

"In fairness, it's not that the governments were unconcerned; these places were just too remote to control. Rubber firms had their own armies. Judges were bribed, inspectors killed, and the Indians were hunted like animals. They'd chain 'em up, take them so far away from home they had no idea how to get back, beat them literally to the bone if they wouldn't work. Maybe tie a couple over an anthill or throw one in a snake pit as an example to the others. These things were common.

"Anyway, the bottom fell out of the rubber business pretty fast." Aterarana smiled for the first time in his story "Somebody finally smuggled out a bunch of seeds, which did great in the Far East, where rubber plantations were a lot easier to manage than in the middle of the Amazon. It's widely believed it was some Dutch guy."

Whitehill returned the smile and shook his head. "That's quite a tale."

"To get back to your question, the Basibo lost a lot of men to the rubber trade. They don't know how we did it, of course, they just know we made it stop."

"And friends ever since," said Whitehill.

"Friends ever since." Aterarana chuckled. "And if you're very good, children, tomorrow I'll tell you about how the high priests of the Incas hid most of their gold when they heard Pizarro had killed Atahualpa."

"What? What are you saying?"

"Later. This is it."

The room swiftly hushed, much like a small theater when spotlights reveal the actors poised to begin. Bandy-legs held his audience easily. As he sang a pleasing tune to a gourd he shifted from hand to hand, many of the Basibo turned to look at Whitehill. They regarded him in the manner of hosts entertaining an odd but popular guest, one whose peculiarities they were willing to humor.

Bandy-legs dipped his gourd into a pot and drank about half a pint. He reached in again, passed the *ayahuasca* to the next man, and so on around the circle, most electing to go back for a second helping. The shaman continued to sing; the men rocked and chanted. Whitehill was aware that the drumbeats had merged into a more serious attempt at rhythm. He joined the undulation, swinging his shoulders slowly in time.

After what might have been hours but was in fact just over twenty-five minutes, patterns in the palm roof started to shift.

They made Whitehill a little nervous. Hoping it was not a breach of protocol, he asked Aterarana if he could catch some fresh air.

The drug began hitting him in waves, but instead of rushing back where they came from, like real ones, these waves remained, stacking on one another, filling the vessel that was Whitehill. He and Aterarana walked a few paces into the woods. The jungle was unusually still. It might have been four a.m. in Peoria. But there was too much overhead, overgrown; always as much as there was on the ground. Drooping, dangling, enclosing. What a treat it would be to stand in the center of a huge, empty parking lot. The thought of it made him dizzy. He couldn't seem to draw in enough air. His mouth was slightly numb, his stomach uncooperative.

The next moment, the forest soared skyward, rearranging itself along elegant lines, graceful arches. Birds nestling in the flowering trees whirled into giant circles of stained glass. Night in the jungle, but Whitehill was in the cathedral at Chartres.

Aterarana touched his arm. Whitehill sensed the muscle strung over the bone, a momentary interruption in the flow of blood.

"Let's go back," Aterarana said.

A soft wind carried them inside. The muddy faces of the Basibo were warm and shy, the hut full of good cheer. Drum rumblings. Bandy-legs swirled designs from Van Gogh's mad period in the sand. Whitehill did not think he could take his place on the mat. The ground was moving. His clothes were moving. But he wanted to join the group and chant and sway with them.

Whitehill sat down and hit the springboard. Delicate cords stretched through time and space, connecting his interior eye to the Siete Chicas bar, to the Lotimone, the Oak Room at the Plaza, the cathedral overlooking Chartres, distant galaxies.

Whitehill wanted a drum. And he felt he was picking up the chants. The hut blinked dark and light. It sounded like someone left a shower on.

He was moving fast now. He shook with excitement. It was a movie. The chief of the Lotimone was in it. So were Avri and Dr. Darreiro. Avri was in a white canoe. Dr. Darreiro was flying. Aterarana was running. Other Indians, too. Whitehill's parents showed up. He explained to them about chanting and being a son and having adventures. They had a nice visit, but the scene dissolved into a nature film. Tapirs, jaguars, anteaters, bats, and birds. A giant anaconda, not slithering, inching forward like a caterpillar, then coiling around him.

Enough of that. Whitehill returned to the room. Everyone was in a different place. Aterarana dreaming into the fire, Bandy-legs pleasantly convulsing in a corner. The first old man had taken up the singing.

Something depressing now. He wanted it to stop. He had to go back. Impatient, anxious. Was this a nervous breakdown? The floor was like death, like a guy he knew in first grade, like a pattern in some woodwork he remembered as a child. Permanent insanity. Each word he thought of melted into any other, making no sense. He focused on smaller and smaller increments of time. His hands were over his eyes. Should he commit suicide? He'd never be the same.

Whitehill popped out, flattering himself on his strength. It wasn't going to happen to him. A peek over the rim, then run like a thief. Saved by the accumulation of experience, by who he was. And humor. "So, Whitehill, now that you've returned from death, what do you want to do?" Who said that?

Moving fast again. Flying. Ah, wonderful. Lifted higher. Over Stonehenge. Over a majestic, flushed granite building that appeared to be a museum. But he was getting too big to fly. The world above which he drifted shrank and disappeared. Retreat to the hut.

The fire threw out an aura of gold, some stars. His hands moved, unbeckoned. Deciding to take control, he grabbed a drum. Everything in here seemed to be circular. Whitehill whipped around to confront a shiny black beetle that wasn't there. He asked the fellow next to him about it, but the voice that came out didn't sound like his own. Moreover, it was almost entirely unrelated to his thoughts. Too crowded in here, maybe. He went upstairs. Upstairs?

Spices and soft music filled the air. He pushed open a door at the end of the staircase. A room with a skylight, another door, frosted glass marked "Private." Within, an old wooden desk, the tops of cargo boats gliding in the windows behind. Photographs, paintings, newspaper clippings on the walls. An arrow leaning in one corner.

Someone in the chair. Whitehill struggling to change places, slip inside. Blurred, strained moments. Sharpness a short way off, a rectangle, the center of its focus. He sensed a barroom down the street, an entire quarter of the city full of bars where his friends waited. Whitehill followed an arm to the fingertips. A pen. With an unexpected shock, Whitehill watched the hand write, "Whitehill watched the hand write."

He attempted to control the fingers and was snapped back into the hut. OK, what happened to his drum? The chanting, the beat accelerated. Sing along for a few numbers, then into the jungle for a little solitude. He left his body behind, skimming through the woods too rapidly for it to keep pace. Whitehill flew into the teeth of a storm, alighting on a nearby boat for safety. The waves threw him from wall to wall, plates smashing on the floor, wind wailing, the deck creaking.

When things calmed, Whitehill disembarked. He had no luggage, so customs let him right through. It was inevitable; he was recognized by someone in the sea of travelers. "It's Whitehill. Hey, Whitehill!" Many handshakes.

A nurse was waiting. She led him down a muddy path into a consulting room. The ceiling was open to the sky; creepers and stray leaves came over the walls. She placed Whitehill in the only chair at a round conference table. A smooth, shining robot was tugging some curtains. Under the nurse's disapproving stare, it waved to Whitehill and closed itself in. The nurse smiled indulgently. She disappeared through a wall of beads that danced and rattled to the conversation that followed.

"Mr. Whitehill is here."

"Whitehill?" asked a second voice.

"That's what I said," the nurse replied. She lowered her volume and buzzed on.

"Ah hah," the other voice picked up, "another 'meaning of life' guy."

The nurse did not reply to this, but Whitehill pictured the same indulgent smile.

"What year is it?" asked the voice.

She told him.

Whitehill could hear papers rustling. "He's not a sociobiologist, is he?"

"No," said the nurse. "Attorney."

"OK. Have old Woody run the audio-visual for me on number eleven."

"Already done."

"And show Whitehill in."

"You know he can't come in here."

"Oh, right. Right. OK, I need a quick drink. Be right out."

The nurse, smiling, parted the bead door. She brushed some nonexistent dust from Whitehill's conference table, straightened folds in the robot's curtain, pushed back the boldest of the encroaching vegetation, and took her place at a small camp stool in a posture of impatient but indulgent forbearance.

Whitehill was slightly amused by it all until the birdman came through the beads. Though a trusting instinct told him everything was just as it should be, the jolt of seeing this pelican head emerging from a full-length white lab coat was not a thing that could be easily discounted.

"Whitehill, right?"

"Yes," returned Whitehill at an octave higher than the one in which he usually performed.

"OK. Batting a thousand." Pelican-man winked to the nurse. "So, Whitehill. Wake up, son. How things going so far?"

"Good?"

"Glad to hear it. Glad to have you here."

"Thank you."

"Woodman, how you doing?" This drew a censorious stare from the nurse. "Not talking, eh?" Pelican-man knocked on the curtain and hit metal underneath. "He knows you're in there. Woody. Say hello." A silver hand flashed out a V sign. "All right, Woodman!

"Now," the pelican continued, telescoping a car antenna and whacking it on the table for emphasis, "pay attention. We're talking billions of years here."

Whimpers of frustration came from behind the curtain followed by the sounds of controls being slammed, drawers crashing shut, and an assortment of miscellaneous knocks. A zing and a purr, and the lights began to dim.

Whitehill felt himself grow smaller. The walls of the consulting room towered overhead until, launching way out of perspective, they ceased to exist. The air was opaque and noxious.

"Prebiotic soup," said the pelican. He waved his car antenna, bringing on sharp punches of illumination. Strange, fluid shapes careened about the room, some knocking apart, some sticking together. Certain patterns of these appeared often and seemed able to make copies of themselves.

"Freeze!" shouted Pelican-man, and the entire room was suddenly encased in a block of ice. "No! That means 'hold it,' Woodman. Back up!"

Whitehill found himself in his parents' first apartment, comfortably settled behind a helping of cookies and milk.

"Too far!"

The shapes returned. They were more complex now, and as this organic gumbo thinned, some of the shapes began to absorb others.

"Please hold it here, Woodman," said the pelican, turning to Whitehill. "That's really all it is. Once these things were able to reproduce, their whole reason for being was to do it—and do it the best way they could. It was reproduce and protect yourself, eat or be eaten. The ones who were best at it were the ones who developed increasingly tough, sophisticated defenses. In short, all plants and animals are just the current model of temporary, protective shells, unconscious of their real function but created by these 'things' over the millennia to act in the way that best ensures a chance of further reproducing copies of themselves into the future. Humans are only robots like the old Woodman here. Automatons controlled from the internal deep."

"And that's life?"

"It explains all behavior on the planet Earth."

The nurse had slowly made her way up to Pelican-man and, at this, delivered an elbow into his ribs.

"Except," said the pelican, "maybe for some environmental influence."

Elbow again.

"Oh, all right. No, that's not quite it. Used to be, though. The difference began when humans got conscious of themselves. A couple hundred years later these 'things,' which you guys call genes, orchestrated this huge cosmic joke where they outfitted their most successful robots—people—in blue denim. Jackets, skirts, bell-bottom, straight-leg, designer, boot-cut, button-fly…all over the world. They went too far. Some humans caught on, and the genes started losing control."

"Wow!"

"Wow? Do you get it?"

"Almost."

"Almost is the best anyone can hope for. Think of it like those old science fiction plots where the computers become conscious of their own existence. Or like Freudian analysis where, when you realize the root of your problem, you solve it. People got smart enough to catch on, take charge. They're really being born for the first time, really free. Let's have some background music, Woody."

"This is not the time for music," said the nurse. "Run him the 'Great Moments in History' show."

"He doesn't want to see that," Pelican-man returned. "How about the first Rose Bowl, 1902? Hey, Whitehill, what's wrong?"

"You have anything for nausea?"

The pelican touched Whitehill's stomach with the tip of his car antenna. "Better?"

"I think." Whitehill shivered. "You know, when I was younger, it was exciting to get close to the truth. Now that I'm older, it's frightening."

"Maybe," said Pelican-man. "The thing about this self-consciousness is that one always feels alone in the last analysis. But you guys are all in this together."

"I still feel that the amount of stuff I don't understand is paralyzing. They add up to a fear that's almost tangible."

"Nah. You're just too late for the ignorance-is-bliss school, is all. You've got to think, but there's no point in trying to rediscover and reinvent all science on your own." Pelican-man walked around Whitehill's table. The waves of the soup were waist high, but his lab coat was unstained. "Forget about trying to understand life all the time. In the context of what you know, try to understand what your life is about."

"You mean I'm not supposed to be upset because these genes are running the show?"

"You're missing it. The wonderful thing about human-ness now is taking that one step away and recognizing it. Standing in opposition to your genes. Acting unselfishly, for instance. Rising above the physical stuff so you can see the humor in life. The magic. Let's have that music now, Woody."

The brass and booms of a marching band thundered out of the curtains.

"We're not doing the Rose Bowl, Woodman. More violins."

"So, what you're saying..." said Whitehill.

"You already know the rest. Beauty, laughter, love, goodness."

"Justice?"

"Yes, of course. Pursuit of truth, knowledge, enlightenment." The pelican raised Whitehill's arm in victory. "Triumph of the human spirit. All that stuff."

Whitehill forced a smile.

"Don't take life so seriously," said Pelican-man. "Do something foolish once in a while."

Whitehill looked at his surroundings. "I think I already have."

The nurse gave a velvety cry of empathy and stepped from her uniform. She came to Whitehill in rosy, Rubenesque splendor, ran her hands over his forehead, kissed him with animal intent.

"Easy, friends," said the pelican. "This has to be good-bye."

The boundaries of Whitehill's world groped back to their original size. Pelican-man, the nurse, and old Woody withdrew, waving, into the past.

"Wait!" shouted Whitehill.

The pelican raised his wing in a gesture of regal hesitation. Whitehill called into the pause, "Is there a God?"

Pelican-man broadened his beak into an amiable grin. "Maybe." He winked.

Whitehill fell into his own body and slept.

THIRTEEN

When Whitehill awoke, it was because his body had used up most of its other options. This was serenity, though perhaps a dose of exhaustion lingered at its core. The day was beautiful. The warm, stifling haze that hangs on after a storm had already been scattered by the late hour. Basibo children bathed in the stream; birds joined in fluting accompaniment.

Whitehill shucked his clothes. He jumped carelessly into the water, let it rock him, float him onto his back. The slow-moving current quickly encircled his face, framing his forehead, cheeks, and chin against the morning sun.

"Hey! Johnny Weissmuller!" Aterarana stood on the bank, beating his chest. "It's the good life, huh?"

Whitehill grinned in response.

"Come on. Get out of there. I've got a surprise for you."

"Another surprise? I've been up for two minutes, and you already manage to ruin my morning."

"No, this is a great one. C'mon up. It's getting late. And be careful…"

"I know. Be careful where I step." Whitehill returned a splash from one of the children, a nod of good morning to some of their elders. He sat on a boulder, knocked the wet sand from his feet, and, at a new level of consideration, stood into his jeans both legs at once.

In the hut, Aterarana handed him a dark, steaming bowl.

"Coffee!"

"That's right, pal."

"I can't believe they have coffee."

"They don't. This is mine. I keep it here."

Whitehill rolled the warmth voluptuously around his tongue. His coffee-starved system rushed the caffeine through slumbering channels.

"Looks like we were the last two up," said Aterarana. "Sleep well?"

"I must have. I feel rested. If your night was anything like mine, so must you."

"Good. You were soaked to the skin. Thought you might come down with something."

"Soaked?"

"Last night. By the time I caught you wandering out in the rain, you may as well have jumped in the river."

"I have no memory of that."

"Don't worry. You were having a great time. Singing 'Anchors Aweigh,' I think."

Whitehill exhaled. "Then what?"

"Nothing really. One of the women gave you some hot broth, and you drifted off to sleep."

"Oh. It's coming back."

"Yucca or plantains?"

Whitehill mechanically grabbed a fat, soggy hunk of yucca. With coffee to wash it down, the bites were almost delicious.

"Take your time, it'll sort itself out when we have a couple of drinks with dinner tonight," said Aterarana.

"Oh, right. Tonight. Canned corned beef. Radio."

"Cold beer."

"Cold beer."

Aterarana walked to the entranceway. He blew a kiss toward a trio of teenage girls staring at him across the compound. They pushed each other and ran, giggling and screaming, into the jungle.

"We better get moving," Aterarana said. "We're getting a late start."

Most of the men were off on the hunt, the women in the fields, but Bandy-legs and a few of the others from the night before had remained to hug them good-bye. In moments, the Basibo were memories.

Whitehill and Aterarana moved into another day. The heat spread back over their path. The sun baked mud to clay; insects hid in the shadows. Whitehill, however, in an elevated frame of mind, bounced and chatted into the afternoon. Crested birds and the giant blue morpho butterflies decorated their way. Whitehill's thoughts drifted into the future, and Aterarana must have caught them as they floated by.

"Going to be sorry to leave South America?" he asked.

"At this point, I think so," said Whitehill. "But if I hadn't penetrated into the interior, I'd have a completely different idea of what it's about."

"Penetrated. That's funny. I always think this continent receives travelers like a small-town Southern whore. Well, I didn't always think that, but at least it's my belief du jour."

"How's that?"

"You know. Flawed, fallen beauty. A little unsure of itself. Suggestions of intimate physical possibilities. The treasure is inside, for a price, which not many are adventurous enough, or foolish enough, to pay. Although everyone basically wants it…and culturally, intellectually a washout."

"Why a washout?"

"Why? Look at Europe. A cerebral penny arcade. Or New York. Crowded, dirty, but no place more stimulating. And what's in the capitals down here? Nothing. Churches. Gold-encrusted altars serving starving congregations. A few good colonial paintings, maybe. But how much inspiration is involved shuffling the location and posture of biblical characters for the ten millionth time?"

"There's more around than just that," said Whitehill, his voice inflating with love and understanding of all mankind.

"Sure, but the rest you see is civilization served up chunk style. A piece here, a smaller piece there." Aterarana stopped suddenly and covered his face with one hand. He dropped his bow and arrows and turned to face his friend. "Whitehill, you're a great guy."

"What?"

"No, you are. All these guys liked you. The Basibo, the Lotimone, even the mole men." He shook his hand.

"That's nice to hear, but are you OK?"

"No. I'm a victim of my own vanity."

"What?"

"Avri was right. I brought you into the Basibo to increase my own prestige. I should have waited or taken you back some other way. Or at least have paid attention."

"Why are you telling me this?"

"Because," said Aterarana softly, "I think we are sur-rounded."

"Surrounded!"

"By Indians."

"Aw. Come off it," said Whitehill.

There was activity under the branches immediately ahead. A sliding silhouette pressed against a tree. Whitehill imagined himself running, but that's not what he did. Rust-lings from behind, a soft bird cry. As his fortunes crumbled, Whitehill instinctively crouched. Silent seconds went by. He became aware of two dark shapes balanced in the giant bush overhead. A face appeared behind the leaves to the left, a whistle from their right.

"Ix-nay the English-ay," mumbled Aterarana.

"What?"

"O-tay e-may."

"Wha! Ha! ha! ha!" Dr. Darreiro. "Ha! Wa, ha ha ha! Caught you. Got you. Ha ha. It took me days, weeks, but I got you. I got you! I knew you'd try to come this way. I knew, ha ha ha. And two of you! Great! This is great!"

Whitehill no longer loved all mankind, especially not these Tsavi. They growled through the nose. Hair, long and wild, fell into unclean smiles. Purple bands around their biceps, red rings painted down each leg.

They advanced from all sides, accidentally bumping Dr. Darreiro in their eagerness. Anger snapped his momentary hysteria. "Idiots! *Ka! Ka!*"

The Tsavi were ordered into action. Coarse loops of twine lashed Whitehill's arms together behind his back. Aterarana, the same. In the pain, Whitehill remembered a cowboy movie where the hero, faced with a similar situation, filled his lungs to lengthen, and thereby later loosen, the bonds. It was unlikely that any of the Tsavi had seen the same movie, but, nonetheless, they sensed his tactic and rewarded him for it with a knee in the stomach.

Whitehill fought, but more out of anger and frustration than in the belief that it would change anything.

"Well now, you screwed up my plans but good," said Dr. Darreiro. "Delay, delay. But I got you. I knew I would." He bent to yell into Aterarana's face. "Hey, boy. Lotimone? Eh? You Lotimone?" One of the Tsavi pulled Aterarana's hair in confirmation.

"Ha!" Darreiro continued. "Well, good piece of work, Whitehill. Stout fellow. You almost made it, didn't you? And still in remarkable shape. That's fine." He began pacing, whacking one fist into the other palm. "You made things rather embarrassing for me back there. Having to explain about Bakiratare and all. Not to mention slowing everybody's plans to a halt."

"Dr. Darreiro," groaned Whitehill.

"Ah, he talks. I was becoming insulted again. It was rude, leaving me so impetuously in the jungle that day. But we're back on the track once again, aren't we?"

"What would you say if I asked you just to let us go?" asked Whitehill.

"What!"

"I'm too numb to think of anything to say except what I really want."

"Too bad, too bad. It's what I want, isn't it?" Dr. Darreiro put his arm around Aterarana's shoulder. "You and Tonto here are in for it now."

* * *

The following days passed in a blur. Was this the fourth or the third? Forced march. Whitehill, yanked from the front, pushed from behind. Hands tied the entire way. Bumping against thorns, slipping through mud.

He gathered that Dr. Darreiro had taken his escape personally. Those times when Whitehill attempted to reason with his captor, he was met with seething silence. Darreiro refused to communicate anything beyond what was essential to their trek.

The Tsavi kept Aterarana and Whitehill separated. During meal breaks they caught each other's eye, but nothing more. If either tried to slide nonchalantly within whisper range, they were whopped soundly for the effort by one particularly large warrior wearing strands of purple, green, and gold plastic beads. By the time they reached the Tsavi encampment, Whitehill had all but given up on the possibility of masterminding his own escape, and he prayed alternately to God, Pelican-man, his genes, Dr. Darreiro's conscience, and the Lone Ranger.

He had been aware for some time of a slow, steady drumroll, and the first villager he saw was the drummer himself squatting behind a set of fat, slitted wooden cylinders. He leered at the prisoner with dumb, malignant satisfaction, grabbed several more sticks in each hand, and flew into a fury of syncopation.

The faces of the Tsavi were without exception unfriendly, some even going so far as to bark and hiss. They did, for the most part, keep a respectful distance. Partly, perhaps, because those audacious enough to come close to Whitehill or Aterarana were sideswiped convincingly by their purple, green, and gold guard. The huts in the village were the most deteriorated and seedy Whitehill had yet seen. A curiously large clean one in the last stages of construction sat dead center in the compound, but everything else looked battered and weather-beaten.

"Good-bye," said Dr. Darreiro, in a way that made Whitehill's stomach rise higher toward his throat than ever before. He and Aterarana were tossed into quarters about the size of two Volkswagens parked back to back. Plants came up through the floor; spiders and cockroaches disappeared into the ragged walls. Mote-filled shafts of sunlight cut through, showing Whitehill what he was breathing and smelling. Odd shapes clustered together, swirling down the smoky length of each beam.

Interesting life. Captured by hostile savages thousands of miles from home, and he sat watching dust. "Hey," Whitehill sighed, "where's the corned beef?"

Aterarana pushed one side of his mouth into a half-hearted smile. "Have to wait for the beer to get cold, I guess."

"Didn't you say something a while ago, something to Avri like 'nothing to worry about'?"

"Did I say that? Optimistic, wasn't it?"

Whitehill was still short of breath from the exertion of the last few days. He made both arms comfortable behind his back and unbent himself against one wall. "Hey," he said again.

Aterarana had been on his knees looking out the entrance. He turned around. "Hmmm?"

"I don't suppose that this is one of your elaborate practical jokes."

"No, 'fraid not."

"And you don't have some surprise escape plan? Something, maybe, that you've been saving up till you could tell me all about it?"

"No."

"Just checking."

"I'll let you know.'"

"Oh, good, good."

The village drummer had strapped on a portable model and was waltzing dramatically from person to person, striking his instrument haphazardly in what seemed mainly an effort to call attention to himself. When he reached the prisoners' hut, he stuck his head through the door, waggled his tongue, and rolled his eyes impressively. When he screamed, Whitehill was so alarmed that he screamed back, and the drummer raced away to the safety of a group stacking weapons in the large, unfinished building.

Anyone not busy with work was busy shouting. Whitehill could see Dr. Darreiro emerging from their midst, but sundown had lengthened the shadows, and it was difficult to make out his expression.

A snarling old man pushed past the guards and peered for a threatening moment at the two prisoners. He dumped a bag of large bones on the doorstep and began pounding them with a rock, depositing the result into a muddy urn.

"Tsavi shaman," whispered Aterarana. "Been known to kidnap children, plump them up, and make 'em vanish."

In response, the shaman growled like a frog. He hobbled off with his brittle, pulverized ashes and sprinkled them into whatever was cooking over the center of the poppy-red fires.

It was possible now to distinguish a high-pitched chant, more animal-like than not, floating over the general din.

Five young warriors danced underneath. When they caught sight of Whitehill, the braves slammed to attention. Each folded into a leaning crouch and, thrusting ahead with rough-hewn spears, marched in unison toward the doorway. When the tips of their lances touched Whitehill's hut, the warriors retreated across the compound and repeated the whole operation, as they and others were to do many more times during the night.

"This is pretty terrible," said Whitehill.

"Nah."

"Oh? For a second there, I thought we were in trouble." Whitehill was deriving a certain amount of satisfaction from his own attitude and did not want it ripped away. Nonetheless, neither he nor Aterarana could ignore the real purpose of events outside their hut.

"War preparations," said Aterarana finally.

"War?"

"Definitely. They'd been quiet for a long time, and we were hoping for the best. But that big place on the other side is only built for the war ceremony."

"Against the Lotimone?"

"That's my guess."

"Won't you be ready?"

"Thanks to you, yes. Even if they came charging in tonight. But they're cunning as well as vicious. Their favorite trick is pretending to be on a friendly mission. Once the other tribe lays down its weapons as a show of hospitality, the killing begins."

"How does anyone ever fall for that?"

"Honoring the guest-host traditions. Sometimes they really are there for a visit or a feast. That and the fact that war in the jungle is more like a game. You know the other guy; you spy on him and try to figure out what he's up to. People die, but not many, and that's not always the object because Indians feel close to their enemies. Family almost. Women and children are usually abducted in raids, and you are never sure if you're fighting a relative. But the Tsavi here," said Aterarana, gesturing to the agitated scene outside, "are into slaughter. Once things are stirred up, anything less than a massacre doesn't count."

Whitehill watched Dr. Darreiro waving a machete furiously in the firelight, cheering on a crowd of dancers. Men jumped, women roared, naked bodies rolled in the dust.

"Well, there's one good thing anyway," said Aterarana.

"What's that?"

"At least we don't have to worry about getting caught."

FOURTEEN

Welcome to Villano, Mr. Tavars. A beautiful city. I am unfortunately unable to see you this evening. We will meet at the air force base tomorrow. I have instructed Elliot to see to your needs.

Cordially,
García

Tavars examined Elliot doubtfully. Quite tall, and to Tavars's mind quite conspicuous, Elliot was dressed in a red plaid cowboy shirt, tight-fitting slacks with simulated paint specks, and high-top tennis shoes. He had done something to his hair that made it look as though he had just stepped from the shower, the grease balling on the stems of his wrap-around sunglasses. It was nine o'clock at night.

Although Tavars had no checked baggage, Elliot insisted on shoving his way importantly into a loud group of German tourists at the claim area. He was there now, beaming back at Tavars as though in possession of some wondrous joke. Tavars disregarded his escort and reread the note.

García always seemed to be avoiding him. Their phone conversations had been short, when Tavars had been able to get through at all. The urgent telexes sent from the States were ignored or handled matter-of-factly. Three times he had received the same reply: "Nothing to worry about." Tavars did not like the way things were working out. They had slipped beyond his control.

And what had slowed down Darreiro, anyway? His last cable from Lomalito had said a matter of days, and it was received weeks ago. He said he'd definitely come up with a fortuitous solution. Then nothing. Tavars could give García no explanation. That in itself was merely embarrassing, but the whole operation had turned dangerous. Extinction by natural causes seemed a failed possibility. He should have made a trip to Lomalito himself, spoken with Darreiro firsthand. But why risk being seen together? Besides, it was sure to be dirty down there, hot.

Perhaps there was still time to reason with García. Abandoning the whole project was the only prudent course. No, he had intended to try tonight, and in spite of mounting misgivings, Tavars knew he must accept circumstances as they stood. These fools down here were too greedy, too stupidly provincial to comprehend the element of risk.

"Ow! Ach!" A scuffle had started at the baggage counter. A very red and round-faced man had put a hammerlock around the neck of a middle-aged woman and was shaking his free fist. Security guards stepped between the couple and...Elliot! The man swore, presumably, in German.

Elliot emerged smiling, blowing lewd kisses at the woman. When he saw the guards had sufficiently restrained the enraged man, Elliot threw in a few ridiculously obscene faces and turned back to Tavars. "No baggage?"

"Elliot, get over here!" What kind of name was Elliot for a South American?

"Yes?"

"Did Señor García say anything else? Was there any other message?"

"Yes."

"Well, what did he say?"

Elliot grinned, but with a little less assurance.

Tavars held up the note. "What else did he say?"

Elliot took the paper from his hand, scrutinized it with a puzzled expression, and handed it back. "For you."

"I know it's for me, you moron."

"Yes."

"Do you know where Señor García is?"

"Yes."

"Well, where?"

"Yes, tomorrow. You come."

Tavars reluctantly followed him to a parking lot reserved for airline employees, where he was dismayed to see Elliot open the back door of a powder blue '58 Chevrolet. A set of huge decals on the rear window spelled out "California University."

Elliot climbed in behind the steering wheel. He opened the glove compartment. A tiny red light inside showed the butt ends of several revolvers. "Guns," said Elliot.

"Very nice, Elliot, very nice." Tavars pretended not to be interested but was unable to suppress a moan. He pushed aside the growing feeling that something would go wrong. "Just take me to the hotel."

"Disco?"

"No, no disco, Just the hotel."

Elliot lifted his sunglasses to wink at Tavars. "Disco?"

"No! Hotel, you idiot." Then, more softly, remembering the pistols, he said, "Just take me to the hotel, please."

"No disco," said Elliot. "Hotel."

"Hotel," repeated Tavars involuntarily.

Elliot drove with one hand constantly on the horn, not an easy trick in a stick shift automobile. They passed under awnings of bright neon, Elliot slowing in direct proportion to the volume of music pouring onto the street. Tavars avoided his wistful glances in the rearview mirror.

Eventually, they pulled into the hotel drive. Elliot immediately began arguing with the doorman over the parking possibilities. Tavars went in to register. His reservation was confirmed, thankfully. No messages. He signed the guest card.

The lobby was animated for such a late hour. Drunken Australians pawed each other in front of the house phones; an elderly, once elegant woman was parading her matched Afghans; two frantic couples herded a brace of youngsters into an elevator; and dark, beautiful women lounged at the bar pretending to attach no importance to the fact that they were dark and beautiful.

Across from the main desk, a miniature jungle wrapped around a semicircle of love seats. In the exact center, under a pair of potted palms, an adolescent girl with too much eye shadow was reading worn copies of *People*. Someone sat on the next cushion, reached over, and turned the page of her magazine. Elliot. The girl looked up in alarm.

"Hello, baby."

Tavars shouted without separating his teeth, "Elliot!"

Casually revealing his chest hair in the best movie star manner, Elliot ambled over to where Tavars had positioned himself in a relatively quiet corner.

"Hello."

"Elliot, look at me." He did. "Now, listen carefully, you moron."

"Yes. Now disco?"

"No."

"No."

"Elliot, you are to drive me tomorrow?"

He flashed a smile of true understanding. "Yes!"

"To the air force base?"

"Yes!"

"Good. Now, I'm going to bed. What time will we leave tomorrow?"

"About two hours."

"No," said Tavars, pointing at his watch, "when? What time should I be ready?"

Elliot shrugged his shoulders. "Maybe one hour one half."

"No. Wait. Let's try this. Will we be leaving before breakfast? Before breakfast?"

"Breakfast?"

"Yes."

Elliot bit his lip thoughtfully. "Probably eggs."

FIFTEEN

Siete Chicas. When the lights faded to brown, Bernardo brought out the oil lamps. He had them burning now in each corner, their flames bouncing, flickering against nightfall in the heat of the narrow, smoke-filled bar.

"It's getting so you can set your watch by these power failures," said McJeffers.

"Ummm." Ryder was studying a map. "Do you carry a watch?"

"Nope. Don't believe in 'em."

"Ummm."

McJeffers traipsed to the counter, crunched out a cigar. Bernardo had a warm bottle of beer waiting. "Where would she get a map like that?"

"Must have copied it from one of García's."

"With details like that of the interior? All those little channels?"

"How else could she get it?"

"That's unexplored territory."

"Not by plane."

"I suppose." McJeffers threw his head back and let gravity deliver the beer down his throat. Stray drops splashed over the sides, joining threads of sweat in the race to his collar. He wiped the back of one hand against his lips. "Where is she now?"

"Got in on the evening plane. She and Boas are at the telex office." Ryder looked up. "Probably waiting for the electricity to come back."

"Umm." McJeffers lowered into his chair. "She quit Aero Amazonia, huh?"

"Same day as her Banco de la Moneda job." Ryder lifted the map. "See where the river splits in here? Must be a lot of current. You could take a boat with a motor, run in upstream, places you could never pole a dugout. Cut off a lot of time."

"Another beer?"

Ryder checked his bottle. "Definitely."

McJeffers turned to Bernardo. "*Dos cervezas más* on Señor Ryder."

"You have a boat with a motor."

"Make that four more beers."

"A big motor. And a shiny new silver propeller."

"I suppose you can borrow my boat."

"That's not quite what I had in mind."

The front door whipped open. Avri walked to the bar and poured herself a *chuchuasco*. Playing Miss Salcedo was getting to be a strain.

McJeffers rose in a rather overdone, genteel manner. The amount of effort this required did not escape Ryder's notice; he smiled but said nothing.

Ryder had willingly allowed Miss Salcedo to entangle him in her plans; he wondered if McJeffers realized he'd taken the hook himself.

"Fucking power failure," she said. "Anyway, Tavars arrived at the Villano airport a short while ago. It's got to be tomorrow."

There was a grunt at the entranceway. Boas put down a medium-sized suitcase. "I thought these were supposed to be portable." He was handed a beer.

Avri looked around the room. "Any of you ever use video equipment before?"

"No problem," said Ryder. "You push a button."

"Indulge me. Practice a bit." She filled herself another half glass and began to pace a tight triangle. "Who's going with you?"

Ryder opened the suitcase, dusted off the camera with his shirttail. "McJeffers."

The round man sat at the sound of his own name. "No way."

Avri turned to Boas. "I'm afraid Señor McJeffers is a more practical choice," he said. "Knows the rivers, speaks some Cofoya. If need be, he can repair the engine."

"No, no, and absolutely not."

Ryder knew that when McJeffers refused in this unqualified manner, he meant just the opposite. By allowing himself to be trapped in such a way, McJeffers could demand dividends of favors and dinner bills for months to come.

"And even if I did agree," continued McJeffers, "the Tsavi are too far away. We could never make it in one day."

"I know," returned Avri. "You've got to leave tonight."

"Out of the fucking question."

"You'll have to excuse Señor McJeffers; he's not himself tonight," Boas said.

"Who else could that possibly be?" asked Ryder.

Miss Salcedo took McJeffers by the hand. "You'll be famous."

"You might even be rich," Ryder declared.

"You might win the Nobel Peace Prize," put in Boas.

"What am I going to do with a Nobel Peace Prize?"

"It pays two hundred thousand dollars."

"Let's not get carried away," said Avri. "I think I can promise you national news, and they'll go at least ten. Twenty if it's any good at all."

"Forget about the money," said Ryder offhandedly.

"Hah?"

"Forget about the rape of the jungle and the innocent lives at stake and think of a big company moving in here with high-salaried engineers and geologists, flashy executives. You'd probably never get laid again."

"Maybe," said McJeffers, "maybe we…"

"What? Call the police? The American consul?"

Avri twanged a centipede off the bar. She smoothed the map at a respectful angle toward McJeffers and perched beside it. Flushed and breathing quickly, she was still self-poised, letting silent seconds fall to her benefit.

McJeffers leaned to Ryder. "Forget the money—figure of speech, wasn't it?"

"Conversational gambit."

"All right, then," said Avri. "You should make the Cofoya by sunrise. Anybody traveling upriver has to go through their territory, and they might know something."

"What I can't figure," interrupted Ryder, "is if this Whitehill guy disappeared a while ago, why do they need the planes? Why hasn't anything started up already?"

"How do you know it hasn't?" asked McJeffers.

"From listening in on García's last meetings. This guy Darreiro has screwed up somehow." She swallowed her drink. "That and the fact that they are loading up bombers tomorrow for somewhere. But double-check what you can with the Cofoya." Avri turned to Ryder. "Did you talk with Señor John again?"

"Yeah. He'll never admit it, but he was definitely lying about taking Whitehill to the airport. He even volunteered he didn't know Darreiro before I got around to asking."

"There is no airline record of Whitehill leaving," said Boas.

"That's got to be it then." Avri grew more intense. "If Darreiro was hired to get the Indians off the land and White-hill suddenly disappears at the same time Darreiro does, he's got to have given him over to the Tsavi. It's just got to be the Tsavi. They would have sacrificed him to the war spirits to ensure victory, then been off and running."

"How do you know so much about the Tsavi?" asked McJeffers.

"Why, mostly from what Ryder told me."

"But how do you account for the delay?" Boas had both elbows propped on the bar. He raised and lowered his shoulders as he spoke. "If there has been no Machiavellian massacre, maybe Whitehill was never with Darreiro. Maybe he's just lost in the jungle. Or dead."

"It's possible, but then why would Señor John lie about taking him to the airport?" Avri hopped off the bar and began to pace again. It occurred to her that if Whitehill had not managed to escape from Darreiro and been found by Aterarana, the Lotimone would now be in the middle of a deadly tribal war. "I don't know what the delay was," she lied, "but it caused them to use the planes and gave us our chance. It's definitely somewhere on this map, and it's probably tomorrow. We've just got to take our best guess." She pointed to a spot on a wide stretch of river. "The Tsavi territory is here."

"Why not some other tribe?" asked McJeffers.

"No. The Tsavi. There's nobody else it could be."

"If there's nobody else, who are they going to go to war with?"

"Well, I mean theirs is the richest land. That's where the minerals are marked. And the oil. And you yourself said they're known to use human sacrifice."

"Didn't García mention the tribes involved?" Boas asked.

"He doesn't know the difference, and he doesn't care. He thought the Darreiro plan was a needless, stupid idea. Nobody bothers with details if it's only Indians being killed. That's more or less a tradition down here."

"Then what's Tavars so afraid of?"

"Someone like us catching them in the act. That's why he wanted to use Darreiro, figure out a quiet way. But García's too arrogant to think he has to worry. He's used to always paying someone off."

"And what about Whitehill?" asked Boas. "If you're correct and he is with the Tsavi, then, presumably, he's managed to avoid being sacrificed."

"Oh yeah, Whitehill." McJeffers had become chiefly concerned with the tiny, blue-winged bugs that always seemed to find their way up his nose this time every night.

"All taken care of," said Ryder.

Avri raised one eyebrow. "You wouldn't do anything to jeopardize getting back with that film. I've got meetings set up tomorrow with the South American bureau chiefs of all three networks. I was planning on promising them delivery in forty-eight hours."

"Well, we'll keep that in mind."

"Look, Whitehill's all right," she said.

"How do you know?"

"I mean, I hope he's all right, but you don't even know for sure where he is. How could you ever find him?"

"If he's anywhere around where we're going, he'll find us."

"How?"

"I have a plan."

"Oh good," said McJeffers. "I always hate to take off in the jungle in the middle of the night through uncharted waters into hostile Indian country without a plan."

"Oh no. I don't have a plan for that."

"No?"

"No, that part's totally up to you. But if we make it in there and get our pictures, I figure we should at least take a stab at rescuing old Whitehill."

"Yes, that's a fine idea," said Boas. "He was an all right fellow."

Avri could not suppress a smile. She thought of Whitehill and Aterarana safely hunched over a warm Basibo campfire. There was a crash of thunder followed at once by rain. The hot air textured to mist.

"Yes, fine," said McJeffers. "This makes it just perfect."

"I'll get you a hat," Ryder volunteered. He plucked an over-size pith helmet off the wall and placed it on McJeffers's head.

"That's not what I need." McJeffers struggled from his chair to the bar. "Something I rarely do, Bernardo. A glass of milk, please."

McJeffers faced the room. His wet, worn safari pants were rolled up, baggy folds hovering in orbit around the ankles; a Hawaiian shirt strained its buttons and hung over where a belt might have been. He listened to the storm beat on the jungle darkness outside. Thick rays from the oil lamps quivered up his shoulders. The fat man in a pith helmet raised his drink between steaming pink cheeks. He belched softly and winked. "To the Nobel Peace Prize."

* * *

The rain had shortened the ceremony, extinguished all fires in the center of the compound. It was quiet, almost cold.

"Hard as it may be to believe," said Whitehill, "I'm so beat I think I can probably get some sleep."

"Do it," returned Aterarana.

He slipped down against the rough, crosshatched wall. "I don't suppose there's much chance I'll wake up in Pittsburgh?"

"No, not much."

Whitehill closed his eyes. "Philadelphia would do."

* * *

Boas escorted Avri to the dock, curious dogs and a pig keeping step. Dim lights and the harsh, fervent music of transistor radios fell back into Lomalito's dark streets.

The storm's last runoff dropped from the trees, drumming corrugated tin shelters built along the shore. A bald, barefoot fisherman curled beside an old woman under one of these. She hummed softly to the water, keeping time with her cane. He worked on a slow cigarette.

There were lines of dilapidated wooden carts parked on a slope dangerously close to the waterline, boats just behind. McJeffers was cursing over his engine; tenacious drops of rain beaded a halo on the rim of his pith helmet. The storm had softened the river, but the big man's movements had his boat bobbing mightily in place.

"What happened to Ryder?" asked Avri, taking in McJeffers's motor with an appraising eye.

"Gone to get his plan." McJeffers looked expectantly at Boas. "Get the ammo?"

"Two sacks," said Boas, hoisting one. "These shells contain an unforgettable mixture of rock salt and sand. No sense killing the same people you're trying to help."

"Aww."

"These others are somewhat more lethal. For defensive purposes."

The squish of mud on the path announced Ryder's arrival. He carried a shotgun of his own, a small knapsack, and a portable tape deck. He stepped in the boat. "I could find only a couple of appropriate selections. College fight songs and a collection of great overtures."

"Better take 'em both," said McJeffers.

"That's what I figured."

Avri stared in disbelief. "A tape player?" Her hair had glossed to wet, sultry curls, dark eyes shining in the flutter of Boas's lantern. "Don't fool around, OK?"

"We have no intention of fooling around," said McJeffers.

Ryder peered down the black river. "How could you, by any stretch of the imagination, call this fooling around? I'm truly hurt. We're both hurt."

"I'm sorry. I'm sorry." Avri switched gears. The suggestion of teardrops appeared over her determined smile. "It's just so important. People like this have got to be stopped."

"Totally and absolutely under control here."

"Absolutely," echoed McJeffers doubtfully.

"OK. Well, stick to the main channels." She bent in and kissed them both with genuine passion. "The river should be wide all around the Tsavi camp. You'll get a clear shot... You did remember to bring the camera? OK. I see it. OK. Just be careful. Please? And come back."

Boas untied ropes fore and aft and tossed them to Ryder. McJeffers fired the engine. "First pull," he yelled. "Not bad, eh?"

Avri raised the tips of two fingers off her lips in farewell and waved until the boat rounded its first bend under the stars. Boas checked his watch. "As much as I hate to bring it up, if you intend catching the plane out tomorrow to spend your weekend facilitating the way with these network people, you'd better get some sleep."

"OK," she said. The motor's waning pops dissolved into the night.

*　*　*

Tavars was unable to sleep. He turned on the television, remembered he was not in an English-speaking country, and turned it off. Room service, no response. Shirt and pants and out the door. The halls were empty; the lobby too crowded. Spying a discarded copy of *People* magazine under a set of potted palms, Tavars seized it covetously, stuffing it under his arm in one quick motion. Back in the room, under the covers, reading light in place, he realized it was the same issue he'd read on the plane three hours ago.

SIXTEEN

The boat bounced in even rhythm as McJeffers hit cruising speed. A choke, a cough, then a deep thrum as the propeller pushed the launch through each surge. Their passage cut a surface of white bubbles, black leaves, and foam holding unknown tangles of worms and fish and snakes beneath. Ryder played a spotlight from shore to shore, resting on any shallow or snarl in their course. The cone of light caught unblinking caimans, the startled flap of bats. Bugs appeared briefly, then were blown into the backwash.

"Hey!" yelled McJeffers. "What's in the knapsack?"

Ryder lifted a loaf of bread and, under that, a bottle. "Present for you," he said, extending them both.

"No thanks."

"It's *chuchuasco.*"

"Nope, don't need it." McJeffers had his right hand on the tiller. In the left, a bottle of his own. "Drunk's the only way to do this," he smiled. "Didn't think your Miss Salcedo would approve."

They drank in unison. McJeffers thought ahead to the swifter currents. At least the night part of their journey was in familiar waters. "Yo!"

"Yep," said Ryder. "Right here."

"I was thinking. You know, even if we hit it just right, make all the right turns, we won't reach the Tsavi until afternoon."

"That's all right. This is the land of *mañana*, remember. García will be lucky to get the planes off tomorrow at all. Afternoon is what she figured on." He turned back to the river. Satisfied with the relative safety of this section, Ryder pointed the spotlight dead ahead, balanced in the bow. He drank, scraped the dirt and possible parasites from beneath his fingernails, and whistled in the darkness.

"Ryder?"

"Yeah?"

"You really think this Darreiro could manipulate the Tsavi into war?"

"Sure. The guy that's got the technological edge has the psychological edge. He can do it."

"But he fucked up."

"Somehow I guess. Maybe Whitehill slowed things down. The real crime now is that we can't stop the bombing."

"Hell, they've been getting away with shit like that for years. You're lucky you're getting this chance."

"I know. Anybody we brought evidence to around here, anybody with the power to do something, is on the take. Or would be."

"And thin evidence at that, to take on the big guys. You're the one would wind up behind bars, pal. You might cause 'em some problems, but you wouldn't stop anything."

"Right. Right. Either we catch 'em making their move, or we got nothing."

A low scream reached out of the jungle. McJeffers held up his bottle, closing one eye to judge the level of *chuchuasco,* which he had lowered considerably. "Hey?" the fat man asked loudly. "Even if we get 'em on film, can't they deny it somehow?"

"They probably will, except a recently bombed-out village is a pretty unassailable piece of proof. But I'm glad you're warming to the consequences of our project."

"You really figure we'll score some kind of journalistic coup, huh?"

"Eh, not necessarily." Ryder squinted appraisingly at twists in the dark jungle wall. The river had begun to tighten. Invisible creatures smelled them pass. Night birds rushed from the engine's growl. "At this point, it's a gamble," he continued. "But we've got who, what, and pretty close to when. If her theory about Whitehill and the Tsavi is right, we got the where."

"Yeah, but why no war yet? Why the planes?"

"Fucked up. Like you said. For some reason, Darreiro just hasn't been able to pull his end off."

* * *

First light caught Whitehill in a depthless sleep. It didn't seem that he had long closed his eyes, but now night was falling away like a slow-moving fog. He shifted. His arms had stiffened, his head had lain too far sideways. Sand pressed thickly into his beard. There was a dream, but he discovered it in transition, and once he moved, it was lost. Someone had been saying, "Your body is the physical projection of your unconscious." Did he have this sort of dream in Pittsburgh? Difficult to remember. There was one about showing up unprepared for an exam, one about seducing a faceless but beautiful woman. There was falling, fighting off attackers, winning a race...

His bones felt heavy against the cramps. Some places were beyond cramps, numb. Whitehill turned to get his blood moving, delivering some life to the dead spots. He thought he was the first awake, but soon there were voices slipping through the whistles and twitters of early morning.

A slight breeze briefly pushed aside the sour smell that clung to the village. Aterarana was snoring softly, the edge of a smile on his lips. He looked like he might have been sleeping off a good bottle of wine.

Whitehill watched small details appear in the walls; then, slowly, he was able to make out faces across the compound. Two Tsavi men ran past, squashing, cracking bugs under their bare feet as they went.

Dr. Darreiro, already moving at top speed, was coordinating a line of workers. They paced off a large circle, marking the boundaries with rocks, bones, strange drawings in the dirt. Cruel-looking weapons were stuck in a jagged cluster at the center.

How long until the sun rose to the treetops? That was as far as Whitehill was able to see. Any place else was a long way off.

* * *

By the time Ryder and McJeffers reached the Cofoya, they were drunk. They had, of course, been drunk when they left Lomalito, but to avoid the chance of a hangover, it had been necessary to drink all through the night.

The Cofoya had no way of knowing this, and the small party that gathered at the shore when the boat arrived found it wise to dive for safety as McJeffers misjudged the speed of his approach. Fortunately, everybody involved in this event found it remarkably funny. When the snickers died down, one of the Indians approached the boat. "Hello, folks."

Ryder had climbed out to inspect for possible damage. He looked back at McJeffers. "What did he say?"

"Ellu fokz," the Indian repeated.

"Hang on here, you speak English?" asked Ryder doubtfully.

The Cofoya were giggling. Their spokesman considered the question. "Shaddup," he said.

Clearly, this was seen as a masterstroke. The rest of the Indians fell to their knees in laughter.

McJeffers's knowledge of Cofoya was limited, and it took him some time to straighten things out. Apparently, two white men had spent the night, but how recently it was difficult to determine. They had, however, been accompanied by a Tsavi Indian, and the Cofoya seemed definite and much more excited about this. Digging through the tangle of interruptions and impenetrable syntax, McJeffers confirmed the information a second time and relayed the crucial points to Ryder.

"I guess she was right," said Ryder. "Goddamn."

"Hoddam," said one of the Cofoya.

"Yeah," McJeffers returned, "starting to look like less of a wild-goose chase."

"Goozjaze."

Two Indians appeared with armloads of fruit. Several more helped dislodge the boat, heaving to inspirational chants of "shaddup" and "goozjaze." Ryder knelt in the bow, juggling two oranges and a banana.

The Cofoya shouted their approval: "Ahh, haii, ooh, hoddam, shaddup!"

McJeffers swung around upstream and left them laughing.

✻ ✻ ✻

"Hello? What's happening here? Hello!"

"*Buenos días*, good morning."

"I need an outside line," said Tavars.

"What number, sir?"

"In Bogotá 24 17 00."

Tavars dug his heel into the carpet, examined the crease in his pants. Circuits crackled into place.

"Banco de la Moneda."

"Señor García," Tavars demanded.

"*Sí, momento.*"

"*Buenos días*," said another voice.

"Is this Miss Salcedo?"

"No, Miss Salcedo is no longer here. Good-bye."

"Wait!"

"*Señor?*"

"I don't want Miss Salcedo. I need to speak with Señor García. García."

"Señor García is not in."

"Has he left any message? This is Señor Tavars."

"No, Señor Tavars. Nothing here."

"Is Elliot there?"

The voice laughed. "You wish to talk with Elliot?"

"He's my driver."

The voice laughed again. "I see. No, Elliot never comes to this office. I will send someone to the garage."

"Please. I'm in Villano. He is supposed to pick me up this morning."

"I will send word. Have a nice breakfast, Señor Tavars. I am sure he will be along presently."

* * *

Whitehill stuck his head out the door. Two spears instantly crossed at neck level. "Hey, guys. All right. Good-looking spears." He turned back to Aterarana. "You think I should take this personally?"

"If it had been me, they probably would have put them right through the throat."

"Oh, maybe not. Communication's an imprecise thing, and you don't really know the Tsavi that well. Maybe all this just means they're happy to see us."

"Aa-uh!" A head poked inside, said something else loud but unintelligible. He raised a machete and with his free hand pushed Aterarana and Whitehill onto their stomachs. There was the sound of more people entering, scraping, snarling disdainfully. The ropes were cut from the prisoners.

When Whitehill sat upright, he was again alone with Aterarana. A bowl of water, a bowl of honey, and a stack of manioc cakes surrounded a large banana leaf on which soft white blobs wriggled in a formless mass.

"Uhh. They look like grubs."

"Excellent, Whitehill. That's what they are. Great delicacy."

Aterarana had begun to knit his brows and slightly nod his head each time he spoke. Whitehill fell this somehow strengthened his friend's nerve. The realization lessened his own.

"Aterarana, do you know why they're holding us hostage?"

"Well, that's not exactly what they're doing."

"Then what are they doing?"

"I think the plan is to kill us."

"What! What? Are you serious? Ooh no. You are, aren't you? Holy shit. Why didn't you tell me this before?"

"No reason for you to lose sleep over it."

Whitehill had been enjoying the honey and was giving serious consideration to a grub. Now the idea was out of the question. "Kill us?"

"Maybe. I think so."

"Kill us. Dr. Darreiro…?"

"Darreiro seems to be working for some company interested in clearing the Indians out of this area."

"Seems to be?"

"Like the chief told you, it's not totally unexpected. We always have people like Avri on the outside, keeping tabs on some of the most likely."

"Oil company?"

"Yeah, and mineral. But these guys get thrown in jail now. Well, once in a while they do. They can't just run wild slaughtering tribes in Indian territory anymore. International protective organizations are watching. The media's hot. Even some new laws. If we're on the land, we have some right to it." Aterarana laughed. "The Lotimone were always good at fighting 'em off though. Do you know they used to try sending geologists in here wearing chain mail armor?"

"And Darreiro?"

"Darreiro reasoned the only avenues left open had to be subtle so nobody gets caught. He wants the Indians to kill each other off or at least decimate each other enough so that we flee our villages."

"What does that have to do with killing us now?"

"Well, he must have been having a tough time starting a war. The Tsavi may be vicious, but they aren't stupid. He can't just walk in and take over. But when he found you, alone and untraceable, he figured giving 'em a plump white body to get them in the mood was a lot more effective than giving 'em machetes and plastic beads. They get a taste of killing and at the same time bring the war gods on their side."

"The war gods?"

"Yeah. Sacrifice. Used to be very important here."

Whitehill fell back against the wall.

"Don't look so shocked," Aterarana continued. "A lot of cultures are taught to believe war is magnificent. Got to appease the war gods to exalt the whole business."

Outside the hut, some of the men had paired off and were applying masks of red face paint. Others pushed and shouted, threatening the sky with raised weapons.

"For the Tsavi," said Aterarana, "a desire to kill large numbers of people, even for no apparently good reason, has always been a highly prized personality trait. They mistake it for strength."

"Why didn't they kill Darreiro?"

"The gifts, and he's probably convinced them he's got shamanistic powers."

"So they want to kill me for starters."

"Um hm. Well, they might give you some chance to defend yourself though. It's not hopeless."

The Tsavi began to gather in larger numbers. White-hill watched the tall warrior with purple, green, and gold beads step from a group of chanters and drink deeply from one of several bowls being passed around the compound. Somewhere the drummer was hard at work. Naked dancers weaved slowly through the circle of stones, sending up small clouds of dust to join the heat of the day.

"You know," said Whitehill, "I was at this party once. I got a little drunk and someone dared me and I jumped off an old bridge into a lake with all my clothes on."

"And?"

"I can remember. I thought that was really something."

*　*　*

"Ohh no. This is really something, now. I can't believe it." Tavars read the note again with increasing fury and frustration.

Welcome to Casado, Mr. Tavars. A beautiful air base. I am at present in conference. We will meet directly I am done. There is a most delightful restaurant across the road. I have instructed Elliot you are to be my guest.

Cordially,
García

Elliot had his own note. He folded the paper several times and snapped it in a shirt pocket under a triangle of imitation pearl buttons.

The room was furnished in a rustic, spartan fashion. Metal tables and filing cabinets, a map on the wall. Tavars looked helplessly at the secretary, a hulking, unsmiling man in a soiled gray-green uniform. Two soldiers flanked a door behind, and a dozen more marched indifferently just outside.

Tavars allowed himself to be led through the white-hot afternoon into the back seat of Elliot's Chevrolet. The trip from his hotel had lasted three hours. Elliot had unbelievably stopped midway to visit a relative, and it was only Tavars's dogged refusal to accept a cup of coffee or tea that got them here at all.

The exit road crossed a central landing strip. Elliot amused himself by drag racing down the runway as planes circled overhead. The Chevrolet shot past the guardhouse and out the main gate, accelerating continually until it reached the gravel parking lot of Restaurante Tres Vidas. An incoming twin-engine bomber swept loudly across, low enough to raise and redistribute most of the dust within a fifty-yard radius. Elliot swore. Tavars coughed and let himself inside, selecting a chair directly beneath the ceiling fan.

After a time, the waitress, and to all appearances probably also the chef, cashier, and owner, lumbered slowly to the table and handed Tavars a six-inch menu. She was a stout woman with a big nose and short hair brushed to the nape of her neck.

Tavars, consumed at the moment by the insulting treatment he was receiving from Señor García, made the mistake of ignoring her.

"*Señor?*" she boomed.

"What do you want? Oh. Not much of a selection. What's this *arroz*? Is that rice?"

"Rice? *Sí, arroz. Con polio?*"

"No. Can't you just wait a minute. It is rice then. What kind?"

"*Qué?*"

"What kind of *arroz?*"

"Kind?" The waitress narrowed her eyes with her patience.

"Of rice. White rice? I won't eat those clumps of yellow rice, and I don't want instant rice, or fried."

"*Señor,*" said the woman, "*arroz es arroz es arroz.*"

SEVENTEEN

"You know, I always wanted my funeral to be a happy affair." Whitehill was sifting sand through his fingers, separating out the stones and popping them in the air. "Cocktails served. A few thousand left in my will for satellite parties attended by those who might find Pittsburgh inconvenient on short notice. Absolutely no speeches from religious figures who never really knew me, but maybe a pulpit where anyone who felt the urge could speak. Or better yet, have it remain symbolically empty."

"Sounds too…" said Aterarana.

"I'm not done."

"Sorry."

"I don't want to lay down rules that are too tight. They ought to play any music they thought I liked, or read something someone remembered I approved of, or tell jokes, or reminisce, or whatever they want."

They caught a glimpse of Dr. Darreiro dragging long flutes in the dirt. He leaned them against the ceremonial war house.

There was a new, deeper pulse to the drumbeats. The Tsavi were vomiting openly in an effort to consume more and more of whatever was in the bowls. They had taken to alternately menacing and embracing each other.

"You're bearing up pretty well, Whitehill. Kind of a brave guy."

"I don't know."

"Sure, you got your jaguar claw necklace there. Banged it right between the eyes."

"Reflex."

"You escaped from Darreiro that time, running alone into the middle of the jungle."

"That was because I realized, all of a sudden, I couldn't stand not being free."

"Hm. Under our present circumstances, that's kind of a bad break."

Whitehill groaned. "I thought you were trying to help. You're not afraid, eh?"

"Well, listen, the Lotimone have always seen death in a different way." Aterarana wiped honey from his mouth. He had thought to bolster Whitehill's spirit, but the guy was brave at that. When Aterarana spoke, he knew well it was more for his own benefit, not Whitehill's.

"You can't really die, Whitehill, because this place itself is alive, and you're always part of it. We think of the earth as just a round plant or a chubby, self-contained animal. Green and wet and wrapped in a protective blue layer of air. Flying around with a bunch of very different, dead rocks in our general neighborhood of the universe. And there's all this tiny, constantly changing offspring it's produced. Moving over or falling back into the soil, floating or sinking in the water. Irrevocable bits of the big process are set in motion as often as someone is born or dies. Everything in and out of the same breathing ball of a warehouse. Unless we blow it up, you're going to be home forever." He checked to make sure Whitehill was listening.

"Of course, since we got smart enough to figure this out, so what? We have to put it all aside to get on with life's real business—the grand games and distractions of love and war, eating and shitting, tipping doormen, and buying real estate." Aterarana looked at Whitehill. "Does that help?"

"No, not really. Good effort though."

"Thanks."

*　*　*

There is an overload point where heat has the power to quiet the forest. But the direct force of the sun funnels between shorelines, following the wandering curves of the river.

The afternoon spilled over Ryder, soaked the back of his shirt. It glittered on blinding ripples, staining the edge of his view.

He reached in the knapsack, pulled out a scarred yellow thermos. "McJeffers?"

"Yeah?"

"Coffee?"

"No thanks."

"It's got cognac in it."

"Toss 'er here."

Ryder handed it over and then turned his attention to the video equipment. Everything tested out, ready to go.

"You believe that theory about drinking hot liquid on hot days cools you down?" asked McJeffers.

"When it's convenient."

McJeffers emptied a full cup and returned the thermos. "Not a bad propeller, huh? Thirty dollars from the old Chinese guy."

"It's got good top end. But these stronger currents are really slowing us down. Think we'll make it?"

"Hard to say since we're not exactly sure where we're going. I'm just guessing at some of these turns." McJeffers glanced at the map again. "We've got to be getting close to the general area, though."

"Hold still. Let's see those teeth." Ryder framed McJeffers's smile against the burning blue sky and ran off a trial shot. Satisfied, he replaced the camera and took a long pull of coffee.

"Any *chuchuasco* left?" McJeffers asked. "My hot liquid theory's not working."

"I'll join you." They drank together. Ryder dragged a red bandana in the water. Sighing softly, he tied it around his neck.

"That cool you down?"

"You bet."

"That's what I thought. You don't look so hot."

"I didn't hear anyone announce amateur hour," chuckled Ryder. "C'mon now. We're losing the mood here." He lifted his tape player onto the seat. "Got to get psyched up."

"All right, always work better to music."

They both laughed in anticipation.

"College fight songs." Ryder looked at McJeffers. "Side one or side two?"

"I can't wait. Whichever one you don't have to rewind," said McJeffers. "Go team. Hey, didn't I hear you tell a woman once you went to Harvard?"

"Umm."

"Wha'ja study?"

"It never occurred to me to study." Ryder snapped in the cassette. "Side one," he announced to the jungle. "All-time favorites." Batteries fully charged, his unit split the air with music, voices bouncing off the hills, the blares, blast, honks, and booms resounding for miles.

Cheer, cheer
For old Notre Dame
Wake up the echoes
Cheering her name
Then the volley of cheers on high
Shake down the thunder
From the sky...

* * *

"Señor García?"

"Colonel?"

"No need to peek through the shades. It is a one-way glass."

"Of course."

García, sniggering, took a last glimpse into the reception area. Tavars was perched on a stool set between filing cabinets. Ignored by the soldiers, he pretended to study a pamphlet on farm machinery that he could not read. Occasionally the silence was broken by dull thunks as Elliot listlessly threw a rubber ball against the building outside.

The colonel was busy over lunch. He was a thick man, one of the manicured, careful sort that unwisely favors a thin mustache. The colonel's hung in prickly contrast over tight, waxy skin the color of dead leaves. With each chew, an interesting collection of scars and blue-black veins appeared on his face.

A half-dressed Indian knelt in the corner, noiseless and rock-still but for the nervous movements of his fingers. Each time the colonel bit into a piece too leathery or too full of gristle, he spit at the Indian, who eagerly gobbled whatever came his way.

"Ah well," García thought to himself, "this is not the city. We must be tolerant of the customs of others."

Three bottles of beer ringed the colonel's plate. Señor García crossed to the desk and placed an envelope against one of these.

"Aha," said the colonel, wiping his hand on his pants. He tore an end of the envelope, sliding out a crisp slab of bills, testing its thickness between thumb and forefinger.

"As per request," said García. "It's all there."

"Certainly. I can count it later." The colonel nodded to his Indian, who gathered the remnants of lunch and left through a back door.

"I have a message here," the colonel continued. "Señor Tavars wishes to see you."

"I'm not here."

"I cannot see you."

"The man's an idiot," muttered García. He lowered himself into a couch. "We could have finished this months ago. With our own methods. The same methods we are using anyway."

"And this man Darreiro." The colonel attempted to catch a laugh in his nose, but García cackled out loud.

"Americans are such fools," García said. "I will never understand their success."

"Bombs are much easier."

"And they might speed along excavations."

They laughed together.

"Ah, García, García, García, my friend." The colonel consulted his watch. "Our planes are ready at any time. Shall we say one hour?" He pushed a button on his intercom.

Moments later, two young women came through the back door, one birdlike and coy, one lithe and unblushing. "You drink cognac, Señor García?"

EIGHTEEN

The drummer rested. For a while, there was only the sound of bare feet as dancers pounded the earth, gradually slowed, then stopped.

Dr. Darreiro watched with absorbed attention. He'd never witnessed this before. The tribe gathered around the circle. They began to hum as one voice, "Eee-eeee-eeeee..." Some shook long, rattling spears; some nervously jumped in place.

The Tsavi were painted red and black. Unnatural, wrinkled shapes rolled over their shoulders, down the thighs. Women trembled their hips under short bark aprons. The youngest among them held armfuls of intense pink and purple flowers. The men wore tight bands at the arms and ankles, most heads crowned with blue and yellow macaw feathers and huge black plumes from an unimaginable bird.

Aterarana was brought from the hut. He was placed at a stake, arms again bound behind his back.

Next came Whitehill. Women screamed. Small children were dragged away. Petals dropped in the dust.

When Whitehill was secured to his stake a few yards from Aterarana, the circle began to revolve. The Tsavi shrieked and stamped the ground. Everyone broke into song, into chants, tears.

They leaped, shouted, writhed in the dirt. The chaos took Dr. Darreiro. He joined the mad twirls, trying hard, but obviously missing the point, like those strangers one sometimes sees at a crowded beach, swimming in their clothes.

All drank. The frenzy thickened; the bowls were filled time and again. Warriors rushed blindly in the crowd, threatening, striking, drawing blood.

Slightly above the ceremony, in a clearing on the hill, the drummer beat time. At the opposite side, where the village met the riverbank, frazzled revelers crawled in the water, dipped their heads, and revived to rejoin the dance.

The chant broke down to wails and growls, and the mood swelled with anger. War clubs flailed the air.

The purple, green, and gold warrior approached Whitehill. A neckpiece of colored stones and snake skeletons had been added over his plastic beads. Whitehill's jaguar claw necklace hung in paltry comparison.

Fresh tattoos had been etched into the warrior's face, interweaving now with a mask of skin infections. Long tassels swung from his ears. He laughed and placed a hand fraternally on Whitehill's shoulder.

Whitehill could count each dark pore under the war paint, taste the man's breath. It was a face cruel and confident, vicious but relaxed, the kind of face you would never follow into an alley.

The man made a sound like a hungry animal discovering lunch. He grabbed a spear from the cluster, ran a step and a half toward Whitehill, and sailed the weapon over the prisoner's head an incredible distance into the jungle.

He turned around to roar his own appreciation, but at that moment a young dancing brave accidentally slapped his nose. With sudden violence, the boy found himself on the receiving end of a wild thrashing, ending, so Whitehill imagined, with the sort of snap a spine might make.

Whitehill caught sight of Dr. Darreiro resting on a stone. He'd acquired a yellow headband and a line of dripping bruises across one cheek.

A thick-bodied straw cylinder, man high, was anchored in the circle's center. Two stout branches were lashed into dried clay at the sides, a nest of yellow feathers on top.

Dull knives sawed through Whitehill's bindings from behind. His shirt was removed; an adolescent girl brought it into the ring, knotted the sleeves around the straw figure. Someone howled, and a dozen spears pierced the cylinder to chaff. The purple, green, and gold warrior stepped forward. He raised a machete to the crowd and brought it down in the same move, neatly slicing off the feathered topknot.

Aterarana's ropes were cut. He was pushed into the circle. Shouts of protestation came from all sides. The tall Tsavi warrior now picked up a huge club laced with sharpened chunks of stone. The roars of displeasure increased.

There was a voice in back of Whitehill. "They seem to want you first," said Dr. Darreiro.

Whitehill almost laughed. "Lucky break for me, huh?" He'd been daydreaming, a land of shining, magnificent beaches where falling snowflakes brushed his face, tempering the tropical sun. With a measure of nerve greater than that required to scale Everest, he took two steps forward. Whitehill was satisfied. He knew he'd enjoyed his life, and nothing more could be expected.

The purple, green, and gold warrior pointed his club at Whitehill's heart. He growled, drooling through a venomous blackened smile.

"Oh, don't worry," urged Dr. Darreiro. "It's just one of their silly rituals. Play along with them."

The Tsavi arranged themselves behind the stone circle, spears and clubs and arrows aimed into the ring. No running out on this crowd. Aterarana was pulled back, leaving only the tall warrior and Whitehill. The adolescent girl emerged from the throng. She walked past Whitehill without hesitation, handing him a scraggly shaft of woven feathers as she went.

The computer shuffled possibilities, options, searched for a plan. Whitehill was not without strategy. He'd noticed that many of the tribe suffered from eye infections, cataracts perhaps. With their corneas clouded, peripheral vision must suffer. He studied his opponent. Both eyes, clear as diamonds, glittered with hate. Oh well.

But there was something else. The Tsavi held his club in the left hand. And Whitehill knew the classic method for handling a southpaw. Circle to the left, always sliding outside the lead foot. The lefty has to reach across his own chest. Then, to win, an opponent concentrates on the left-hander's right.

The purple, green, and gold warrior raised his free hand to his teeth, bit off a hangnail, and transferred the club back to the right side.

Well, one strategy left. Whitehill pretended to drop his feathered truncheon. He retrieved it quickly, while surreptitiously squeezing up a scoop of loose dirt.

"I will show you fear in a handful of dust." No, not quite the right interpretation. Whitehill laughed out loud. This disconcerted everyone, especially Whitehill.

Nothing funny here. He was up against a man with the body of a broad, acrobatic ape and the face of a mongrel. To Whitehill, the warrior might as well have been a huge animal, powerful, unreachable with words.

As the Tsavi began to move, Whitehill was sharply aware of the man as a gathering of sounds, scents. What to watch— the eyes, the feet, the hands?

The warrior breathed faster; a tiny brown wart swayed on his ribs. The drummer played with rapid intensity; the circle bobbed and shouted.

Whitehill backpedaled as the blades of the club blew past his eyes. The purple, green, and gold Tsavi handled his weapon like a matador, cutting a graceful letter S in his follow-through. He lunged again, an edge this time slicing through a front pocket of Whitehill's pants. The next nipped a sliver from his forearm.

A collection of internal alarms rang in Whitehill's head. He moved instinctively; he was light on his feet. In the blur of the crowd, a large-breasted woman blew her nose into her hand. Two small boys fought for possession of an arrow. The corner of Whitehill's eyes caught Darreiro, Aterarana, the spinning backdrop of trees, river, hillside.

For lack of anything else, Whitehill still held his feathers. He used them to block his opponent's field of view. He pivoted. Points of the club swirled where certain important areas of Whitehill's brain had been a split second before. The warrior went for his face, a tip nicking a tiny freckle of blood from the end of his nose.

Whitehill was having some success, but all on the defense. Even so, not too bad. He swaggered, he was jaunty, he moved like a cagey welterweight. Another swipe, a clean miss. Whitehill was seized with an exhilarating sense of abandon. The Tsavi's grin began to harden. Whitehill threw his dirt, a fist right behind. Indians may know the dust-in-the-eye trick, but it is a fact that they don't punch very often. Whitehill selected an uppercut, a blow with a high percentage of landing somewhere. The warrior, temporarily blinded, instinctively bent forward to rub his eyes. He took it on the chin, his head snapped, and the ground came up underneath.

Had this been a movie, the man would have been knocked out cold. Unfortunately, what happened was, it made him mad.

Whitehill, never having killed anyone before, wondered if that was his only way out. The moment passed; he lost his advantage.

When the Tsavi stood, Whitehill had a sinking suspicion that the warrior had only been toying with him to delight the crowd. Now, suddenly losing both the fight and his sense of theater, the Indian narrowed his eyes with furious intent. He rushed at Whitehill savagely.

But amazingly, he stopped. Then Whitehill heard it, too. From deep within. From out of the past. It was unmistakable. The sounds of rescue. It was horses, maybe. It was French horns, violins, flutes, trumpets. It was a cavalry charge.

The Tsavi broke ranks and walked in silent wonder to the riverbank. Music, an orchestra, gaining strength, galloping, resounding, then a final crescendo falling into the low throbs of an engine.

Voices carried over the water.

"Hey, great. What was that?"

"'Light Cavalry Overture.' Ya liked it, huh?"

"Let's hear it again."

"No. Twice in a row? I'm switching back to the college songs."

"Where's the *chuchuasco*?"

"I thought you had it."

"Oh yeah."

"So, whaddaya think? Too much bass? I got the volume on nine. Never had it over five before. Think I can still pump the sound a little. Maybe with the old treble knob."

"Hey, hold the boat straight!"

"You're steering," Ryder laughed.

"Oh, yeah."

Ryder popped in the next cassette as the boat nosed into view from behind a point of trees. "Pass the bottle."

"Uh oh."

"Hmmm?"

"Just turn around and smile."

"Ew."

McJeffers waved jovially. "Tsavi," he said through his teeth. "This how the plan was supposed to go?"

"Well, you can't have expected me to work it out to the last detail."

The Indians drew their bows, shouldered their spears.

"Hang on. Is that Whitehill back there?"

"Goddamn. Unless the Tsavi been shopping at Brooks Brothers."

They drifted closer. McJeffers clicked off the safety on his shotgun. "I can't say they look friendly."

"One of us better check. I'll drop you off."

"Bad idea. Got to hand it to you about the music, though. He heard us, all right."

"Everybody heard us. That's the problem."

The Tsavi's curiosity about the boat was turning swiftly to concentrated hatred. Whitehill, disregarded for the moment, took tentative sidesteps toward the general cover of the jungle.

There was heated discussion among the Indians. Some held their weapons trained at Ryder and McJeffers. Some made for the canoes.

"We're coming well within range, you know."

"I haven't been able to think of anything else."

The Tsavi yelled; Ryder saluted back. "Don't let that engine die."

"Don't say die."

Whitehill had made definite progress. Humming softly, hands folded nonchalantly behind his back, tipping, toeing out of the circle of stone.

"No!" Dr. Darreiro broke the spell. He screamed. Whitehill ran; half the tribe took after him. For a few seconds, he became the fastest man alive. It was like shooting through a bobsled run. His balance was perfect. He looked over his shoulder, saw a stampede of Indians. Suddenly, his knee hit something hard and he bounced off into the jungle.

Arrows were loosed at the boat. Scrambling, shouting warriors launched their canoes. Ryder hit the tape.

Cheer, cheer
For old Notre Dame…

McJeffers fired a round in the air. Whitehill raced between the leaves, a diagonal, heading for where the boat would be in a minute. He could feel the screaming Indians on his back. The forest filled with pandemonium. Spears whizzed past his cheeks. Splinters of wood, smashes of dust and leaves tore on all sides.

The canoers had been momentarily confused by the music. Now they were regrouped and paddling furiously.

McJeffers ran the boat ahead, but it was touch and go whether they could grab Whitehill and still save themselves. He tried to remember how long ago he'd filled the gas tank. The Tsavi were catching up to Whitehill, closing on Ryder and McJeffers.

Then the sky began to change. An overpowering threat roared up from the horizon. The planes came in low, two of them in single-file formation. For a moment, Whitehill thought they had come to save him. When the first bomb hit, he was knocked to the earth. Dazed, nearly panicked, he almost ran back to the village.

Ryder's camera caught them passing over. "OK, a wide one now! Pull over to the far bank!"

"What about Whitehill?"

"We can get him in a minute."

The next bomb landed in a crowd, spouting blood. A whistle, then a clouded burst of fire. The percussion leveled the war hut, threw Darreiro off his feet. Screaming children hid beneath their mothers. Another blast, the ground turned upside down. The water foamed. Rocks and dirt, pieces of trees rained into the boat.

"Holy shit!"

"I think I got the wing markings. Keep it steady."

"It is steady. You're what's shaking."

Direct hit, the village seemed to fly apart. In terror, the wounded broke for cover.

McJeffers shot vainly at the sky. "Assholes!"

The Tsavi swarmed across the clearing, the chaos of an anthill kicked open.

And Whitehill was losing his lead; the arrows came faster. He was in the river, roiling now, full of darkness and debris. There was a clapping noise, and he threw himself under.

Shafts cut skinny torpedo lines through the water. Whitehill swam wildly for the depths. The bottom shook, tossed him up.

Old Notre Dame will
Win over all...

The boat. The Indians. A spear zipped by. An explosion behind him. The jungle lit orange. Hot roaring winds shoved down trees.

"Over here! C'mon, Whitehill. You got it." The Tsavi were too close.

A hand on the boat. Whitehill looked up into a camera lens. Aterarana surfaced beside him. McJeffers swung his shotgun around. Whitehill grabbed the barrel. "He's with me!"

"Gimme your arm."

"Look out!"

Boom.

Whitehill hooked up an ankle.

"Watch it."

"Quit rocking the boat!"

McJeffers hit the throttle.

* * *

And that, of course, is how Whitehill became famous. As it turned out, Ryder had talent as a cameraman. Heart-stopping clips of Whitehill's escape and the attack on the Tsavi village were shown on national news three nights running. *Newsweek* selected a shot of Whitehill swimming from a backdrop of charging Indians and detonating bombs for its cover. The resulting publicity focused world attention on the plight of the South American Indian. *Time* had no choice but to retaliate by naming Whitehill Man of the Year. Invitations came in from TV talk shows, and he accepted them all, as well as dinner at the White House and Buckingham Palace.

His speech at the United Nations was so favorably received that international pressure shamed several Latin American countries into rushing through laws, forever securing land rights for their indigenous populations.

Whitehill was installed as an honorary member of the Explorers Club. He was invited to speak at Notre Dame's graduation ceremonies. The Rolling Stones wrote him a song.

He was recognized in restaurants, taxicabs, elevators. He threw out the first ball at the Pirates' home opener.

Kids all over America bought colored T-shirts with logos of little white hills. Women bribed hotel clerks to sneak into his rooms.

Eventually he married one of them—a French film star who also made the cover of *Newsweek* when she gave up her career.

McJeffers and Ryder had their share of fame as well, accompanying Whitehill to the Explorers Club, *The Tonight Show,* and Notre Dame. When the action died down, McJeffers capitalized on his natural proclivities and grew rich exporting *chuchuasco.* Ryder was unable to improve his relationship with Miss Salcedo and eventually retired quietly to northern California. McJeffers comes to visit from time to time on his promotional tours and the two sit among the redwoods, laughing and drinking up the free samples.

The Lotimone continue to live peacefully in an unexplored, unmarked region of the deep jungle. Avri never married but became mother to twins and is the first woman hunt chief of her village. The mantle of full chief fell to Aterarana, who still makes trips out and can sometimes be found, in his secret identity, drinking and inventing jokes in New Orleans's old French Quarter.

It was the Tsavi who became well known. Two members of the tribe now serve in their local legislatures. The purple, green, and gold warrior with whom Whitehill became so intimate went on to win an Olympic bronze medal for javelin.

Only Tavars and one of the bomber pilots received prison sentences. García and the colonel retired to Switzerland and Paraguay, respectively. Elliot, only dimly aware of the whole affair, and of all the events swirling around him, was nonetheless able to sell an inflated version of his involvement to a large newspaper chain. He had the story laminated onto the hood of his Chevrolet. Girls like it.

EPILOGUE

Many years later, Whitehill's law office, Pittsburgh. Whitehill is reclining in a brown leather chair, relaxing with a snifter of *chuchuasco* after a hard day's work. On one wall, a huge Audubon print of the Louisiana pelican is flanked by honorary diplomas and photographs: Whitehill in a golf foursome with the last two presidents and a governor, Whitehill in a hard hat with the Prince of Wales, touring a steel mill. There is a jaguar claw necklace draped over a bust of Clarence Darrow.

The door opens admitting a strange, warm breeze. Papers rustle on the desk.

"Mr. Whitehill?"

"Yes, Carol?"

"I'm sorry to disturb you, but there was a funny old man here."

"Yes?"

"Well, he left this package for you. I said I didn't think you were busy and I'd buzz you, but he didn't want to stay."

"Not busy?"

"Well, you know. And he insisted I bring it immediately."

"OK. Thank you."

It was a rectangle of brown paper, a book. Whitehill unbent his Swiss Army knife, cut the string, and tore away the wrapping.

Plants and Insects of the Amazon by Dr. A. K. Darreiro.

ABOUT THE AUTHOR

 James Polster is a novelist, journalist, and movie producer who earned graduate degrees from Harvard University and Columbia University. A National Fellow of the Explorers Club, he has traveled the world profiling international luminaries such as Indira Gandhi and Donald Trump and covering such major athletic events as the Duran/Leonard Superfight and the World Championships of Elephant Polo. In addition to *A Guest in the Jungle*, which helped focus a spotlight on the disappearing Amazon rain forest, he is the author of *The Graduate Student* and *Brown*, which was named by *Publishers Weekly* as a Best Book of the Year.